The School of Women

Dialogs 1-5

Nicolas Chorier

Translated by Richard Robinson

Sunny Lou Publishing Company
Portland, Oregon, USA
http://www.sunnyloupublishing.com

2nd Edition: April 23, 2024
Original Publication Date: October 27, 2021

ISBN: 978-1-955392-68-6

The details of the French edition of this work, from which the English translation was made, are unclear. Original authorship in French is attributed to Nicolas Chorier (AD 1612-1692).

Contents

Foreword

The School of Women from the 17th century was a romp to translate the first time around. Two and half years later, in order to detect and correct any infelicities that might be lurking in the original translation (and there were not many, but there were quite a few[1]), I had to re-read it. I confess that it took a lot of courage and effort on my part (and a long time) to get around to it – for my heart wasn't into it. But on a re-read finally (and review) I found, much to my delight, that the novel is much funnier than I remembered. How can it not be funny: at a certain point all the sex that happens becomes simply ludicrous. People in life just don't have that much sex. Or do they? I don't know. Or maybe it was a 17th-century France phenomenon. Or maybe a European phenomenon among the upper classes. I cannot say for sure (for I haven't done any research into it).

Someone once asked me how much literary merit *The School of Women* had. "Not much," I admitted at the time. The other person scratched his beard in response, if I remember correctly. But it *is* funny, and that has got to be worth something!

The original reason for translating it was not for any literary merit it might have, although on setting out I probably hoped that there was some – but because of a scene in *Theresa The Philosopher,*

---

[1]No translation is ever quite finished. There is always some improvement to be made. The same is true for proofreading: try as one may, there is always one last typo to be found and corrected.

wherein, towards the end of the story, the serial masturbator female protagonist succumbs to her desire and consequently loses her bet with her beau, the count, not to masturbate, thereby gaining the ultimate happiness in life – a long and successful relationship. There is mention of a series of libertine novels and stories that she reads prior to the denouement and her "down fall," together with several erotic paintings on the wall (all lent to her by the count) that she admires. Among the books she read, there was *The Academy of Ladies*, here translated as *The School of Women*. Call me a completist, or call me curious, but I had to translate it (at least in part). Maybe someday I will muster the courage and strength to translate the last 2 dialogs.

If there is any lesson to be learned from not a few of the many French libertine novels, one stands out to me. That although the French of the 17th and early 18th century were not always faithful to each other in marriage, they understood the value of keeping up appearances – for the good of society. I believe they meant it. *The School of Women* (at least the first 5 dialogs of it) and *Theresa The Philosopher* both have this same message.

Today, it seems, at least in the United States of America, if not Europe, we look down on such a message as so much "do as I say, not as I do," which moderns hate. But do we really have the right attitude?

– Richard Robinson (2024 April 23)

First Academic Dialog

Players: Octavie, Tullie

Tullie.

Hello, Octavie.

Octavie.

At your service, cousin: I'm delighted to see you; I was just thinking about you.

Tullie.

I come, my dearest, to rejoice with you, about the news I just heard, about your marriage to Pamphile: I have to say, as a friend, that I am as much taken with it as if I had to share in your pleasure, on your wedding night. Ah! My child, how happy you will be! You deserve the most tender caresses of a husband, on account of your beauty.

Octavie.

I'm really obliged to you, cousin, for the interest you take in my affairs: I expected nothing less of your friendship; & I'm delighted that your visit gives us the opportunity to discuss this subject fully. I learnt yesterday from my mother that I've only two days to go; she's already set up a bed, & prepared, in the cutest apartment of the house, a room, & everything necessary for this celebration. But to tell you the truth, my dear Tullie, all these preparations give me more fear than joy; & I can't even conceive of the pleasure you say I ought to receive.

Tullie.

That is not very surprising, what with your being young & tender (for you only recently celebrated your fifteenth birthday), – you have no idea of the things that were entirely unknown to me, when I got married, although I was a little older than you. Angélique was telling me often enough, that I was going to enjoy the most delicious pleasures in the world; but alas! my ignorance made me deaf to all her words.

Octavie.

You surprise me, Tullie, & I'm having a hard time believing what you wish to convince me of, regarding your ignorance. Do you think I don't know that you've always passed for one of the brightest girls of our sex; that you're known to be knowledgeable in history & in foreign languages; & that your active mind could not have escaped intimacy with the most recondite things in nature?

Tullie.

It is true, Octavie, that I am particularly obliged to my parents for having raised me in the study of everything that is the finest, & most curious, subjects to know about; I also pushed myself to accord perfectly with their intentions: for far from glorifying my learning & my beauty, as is common among girls of our sex, I have avoided splendor & love affairs like a dangerous reef, & done all I can to acquire the reputation only of a wise & honest girl.

Octavie.

Those who've no intention of flattering us say there's nothing rarer than a learned & enlightened woman, who keeps within the bounds of honesty. It seems to me that the more knowledge we take in, the less virtue we have; & I remember, Tullie, having heard you discourse on that same subject recently, which goes against the affectation you've just shown in describing your conduct. For, let's be frank here, is it really possible that your beauty, capable on its own of inflaming hearts, has never encouraged you to participate in diversions you couldn't resist? No, I can't be persuaded, inasmuch as your mind itself should suffice to engage those blind enough to be insensible to your face's features.

Tullie.

How is that, Octavie! Where is your simplicity of just a moment ago? The word marriage makes you afraid; & now you are talking about love, beauty, & diversion! You know what it takes to engage a heart, & your mind is sharp enough to discover what I wanted to conceal from you. I will tell all, given you have been adroit enough to penetrate my heart's feelings; I do not want to make a mystery of anything anymore to you: no more smoke & mirrors. I ask only that you show an ingenuity equal to my own, & that the confidence you place in me in your displays of friendship are sincere.

Octavie.

Ah, Tullie! The difficulties a girl in love has to keep hidden from the outside what goes on inside her! No matter how you disguise your words, I can see through your eyes the movements of your soul; & the sympathy that exists between these two parts helped me to understand the truth. Once again, then, be more sincere & more honest with me, & do not abuse the credulity of a girl like me. If you ask me to, I'll open up my heart to you as if to my bosomest buddy; & so that you might have no doubt about it, I'll give you some proof, by telling you about what happened between Pamphile & me.

Tullie.

I love you with all my soul, my dear child; & the confession that you have just made with such tenderness of feeling, encourages me to cherish you all the more: let us hear it.

Octavie.

As you may know, Pamphile has come to my house quite often; he's paid me many a visit, & I've always noticed in his behavior the true impulses of a man possessed by love: but for some time now he begins to be more bold with me; & the assurances he received to marry me did away with all the fear he had previously. One day, among others, he threw himself at me with such impetuousness, that I was taken aback; he kissed me with such warmth, that I was all aflame, & I can't conceive of the reason for these quite extraordinary actions.

Tullie.

Sempronie was not present? You were alone, & you were not in the least bit afraid of Pamphile?

Octavie.

Yes, my mother had gone out of the room, & I don't know that I had any reason to be afraid of him.

Tullie.

So what is it that he needed, some kisses?

Octavie.

I can't say that he received a single one, he stole them rather; he took several, with much feeling, sticking his tongue amorously between my lips.

Tullie.

And how did that make you feel?

Octavie.

I have to admit that I felt a certain unexpected warmth, that set me all ablaze; all parts of my body were animated; & the warmth that mounted to my face helped me to do away with that importunity of his: he imagined it was an effect of my modesty; & that's why he gave me a moment of respite, & took back his hand.

Tullie.

Go on; go on; what was he doing with his hand?

Octavie.

Ah! I'm not a fan of those thievish hands of his, always moving around & so active! They kindled a fire under me, judging by the heat I felt. At first he slid them into my bosom, where he pressed my tits tenderly; & laughing while speaking, he said he found the first one as firm as the second; then he pushed me onto my back on the little damask-upholstered couch we were sitting on.

Tullie.

Ah! you are blushing, little cousin; Am I to understand that you were taken?

Octavie.

Holding me with his left hand, all my efforts to resist were useless (I'm telling you these things as they happened); then he slipped his right hand under my skirts, & all of a sudden... ah! I'm ashamed to say it, I can't tell you the rest.

Tullie.

Oh, Gods! Are you still so timid & so foolish as to be afraid to tell things like they are? Chase that fear & that imaginary modesty far away; there is nothing so ridiculous in a person who professes to be wise: go on then, & just keep in mind with whom you are speaking.

Octavie.

Soon thereafter he pulled my skirts up to my knees, & stimulated me by touching my thighs. Ah! cousin, if you'd seen him at that moment, you would've admired him; he was red in the face, like fire, & all his actions were accompanied by such heat, that you would've been surprised.

Tullie.

Sounds like you were enjoying yourself in this little pleasantry, & that these sweet pastimes gave you some pleasure!

Octavie.

Having then brought his hand a little higher, he took possession of that part of our bodies that distinguishes our sex, & which each month releases, in me for a year now, a large quantity of blood for several days on end.

Tullie.

Good job, Pamphile, good job; go on then, cousin, your story has promise.

Octavie.

He's really bad, Tullie; after hurting me several times by rubbing me & touching me, just about everywhere, he said to me: "Ah, my love! Ah, my dear Octavie! It's this part here that will give me happiness; allow me, my love, to just...." I thought I was going to faint when he said this: that place, Tullie, has a small, bright-red slit; he put his finger in it; but it was too tight, & I felt a sharp pain.

Tullie.

And then, what did he say?

Octavie.

At the moment when the pain he was causing me with his finger made me let out a few sighs, he exclaimed: "Ah, she's a virgin, it's a virgin I will have have the pleasure of enjoying! And with that, he pried open my thighs, which I was squeezing tightly together as much as I could, & he leapt onto me, as I was lying flat on my back on the couch.

Tullie.

And then what happened? You are not speaking; did he put only his finger in that place you mentioned?

Octavie.

Ah! I felt... but I don't dare say it.

Tullie.

Come on; you are acting silly! What happened to you then has happened to me as well. There is nothing so brazen as a desperate husband, when the enjoyment of a good that was promised him is delayed; he is always in a state of anxiety, & can find no rest, until he has plucked, or rather torn to pieces, that flower of our virginity.

Octavie.

I felt then, between my thighs, something, I don't know what, hard & heavy & full of heat: he pushed it into that slit with a great deal of violence; but summoning all my strength, I rolled over onto my side, & I got rid of him by this means, while placing my hand over that spot where he wanted to enter me.

Tullie.

What! You were able with your hand to ward off so great a stroke, & to fell so great a Knight? You will not always be so strong.

Octavie.

Yes, I did, cousin. "Ah! You're vicious," I said to him, "what makes you want to cause me so much harm? What did I do to deserve such bad treatment?

Ah! If you loved me, Pamphile!..." And on saying this, I cried, & I was very upset, so that I didn't recognize myself any longer, & I was barely in control of myself.

Tullie.

Pamphile, then, was unable to pierce you with his pike, nor to make himself master of the citadel?

Octavie.

No, because I warded off the blow; but alas! If you only knew, Tullie, I suddenly realized that I was completely drenched (naked as I was to the navel) as if by a downpour, which the sun had warmed: I put my hand imprudently on that "place"; but I'd have rather not touched that liqueur, that Pamphile's fury had got me all wet with, when finding it thick & viscous, I imagined... I don't know what horror.

Tullie.

So neither of you were the victor?

Octavie.

I believe Pamphile had the advantage; for since that time, he's ever present in my thoughts; he seems more lovable & more agreeable to me than ever before. This disturbance & this disquietude prove to me that he came away the victor; I burn with a secret & hidden fire, that I can't extinguish; I don't know what I desire, I can't express what it is that I want: the only thing I'm certain of is that of all men, he's the one I've the most feelings for; he's uniquely dear to me, & it's from him alone that I wait for more pleasures & delights, that I can't even conceive of: but, alas!

Will you believe it? I can't stop, in my ignorance, desiring him passionately.

Tullie.

Has no pleasant dream charmed you while you slept? Have you not at all dreamt that you were enjoying your lover's embrace, & that you have already shared with him the sweetness Hyman prepares for you?

Octavie.

There's no need for me to lie to you, cousin; night & day I've Pamphile's image before my eyes, & that imaginary presence has sometimes caused me during my sleep unbelievable voluptuousness. But alas! When I reflect on it, it's like chasing after a phantom, searching for pleasure in the imagination; I'd have rather recovered the occasion I lost by my stupidity, by refusing him what he wanted from me: but alas! There's no point anymore of hoping for anything from that quarter.

Tullie.

And why is that? Can you not see him today or tomorrow?

Octavie.

No, that can't be; & here's why: you know, Tullie, that when Pamphile & I were alone together playing around, I had only just put down my skirts, & he had only just tucked in his shirt that was hanging out, when my mother came into the room, & surprised us.

Tullie.

Ah! I am afraid for you! Because I know Sempronie's

temper.

Octavie.

She didn't say anything to us, however, that would have given us notice of her anger, not to Pamphile nor to myself; she asked us only, while laughing, what we were talking about, & which of us two loved the other more tenderly: because the person (she continued) who most deserved to be loved, – "I've no doubt, that it's you, Pamphile, & I believe that Octavie will not dispute you in this matter; nonetheless I desire that since marriage must unite you with my daughter, that you should display only friendship for her, & that your natural goodness should draw from you the affection that should be a result of her desert."

Tullie.

All that was said in front of your lover; but after he left, then what did she say, nothing?

Octavie.

He'd just left when she interrogated me on what she'd seen of us both; I did what I could to excuse myself; but she made me confess the truth. I pleaded with her then to see that Pamphile had almost oppressed me by his violence; but that I was ignorant of what he wanted, & what he was looking for; that for me, if I had committed a sin, I didn't know in what. She asked me, if he hadn't violated me; (that was the term she used): I told her no. "You should know, daughter" she continued, "that in a short period of time you will be Pamphile's wife: if you were so complaisant as to give him beforehand what he desires from you, then you would afterwards be the most miserable girl in the world; for it is certain that he would abandon you: & if after that he should be constant enough to take you for his wife, he would have nothing but contempt for you." From this day forward, it was impossible for us to find ourselves alone.

Tullie.

Sempronie was right; for a young man, no sooner has he tasted the pleasures of love, by enjoying the caresses of a girl, than he conceives disgust, from the moment he has received her last favor: but I praise your ingenuity & the candor with which you have told me all this; you will lose nothing by it, & you will discover in me a naivety to rival your own. Sempronie pleaded with me yesterday to instruct you in all the most hidden secrets of marriage, to teach you how you should act with respect to Pamphile, & what his prerogatives & his advantages are. It order to do this, my dear, we must sleep together this evening; I will act like your husband, & you will act like my wife – in anticipation of the time when someone else will make you enjoy more solid pleasures.

Octavie.

That would be wonderful, cousin. There's no better way for me to employ my time between now & the wedding, than in the study of the science that is at one & the same time so necessary & so unknown to me.

Second Academic Dialog

Players: Octavie, Tullie

Octavie.

Well, Tullie, here we are lying in the same bed together: you've been looking forward to this moment for a long time now; & the absence of Orante, your husband, has succeeded in bringing it about according to your desires.

Tullie.

I cannot tell you how happy I am: it is enough to tell you that I am burning with love for you, & that the intensity of this passion has caused me to pass many a sleepless night before now; my grief was insupportable, being unable to enjoy, as I so desired, the object I cherished more than myself.

Octavie.

But, cousin, I think that if you were desiring me for so long, you don't love me less at present.

Tullie.

Yes, my love, I love you, or rather I languish & die of love for you; & I can even assure you that my passion is equal to that of Pamphile's.

Octavie.

What do you mean by that, cousin? Because I can't

conceive how the friendship you have for me is any-thing like the love Pamphile can have for me.

Tullie.

I will explain it to you; but before I do, drive that shame & puerile pudor far away, as they can get in the way of the enjoyment of our discussion.

Octavie.

Haven't I already laid aside all my timidity, given that you desired me to lie completely naked in your bed, & I obeyed you? Isn't it enough that I've gone to bed with you, in the same spirit, as if I were with Pam-phile; & that I've promised you that you would find me as docile as a novice?

Tullie.

According to my desire. Well then, the first proof of your obedience is to give me a kiss, but a kiss from the heart.

Octavie.

I'll give you not just one, but a thousand, if you like.

Tullie.

Ah, gods! What a divine mouth you have! And how your eyes shine! & the shape of your face is beautiful, just like Venus'.

Octavie.

But what're you doing, you've thrown off the bed-sheets! If it wasn't you, Tullie, I don't know just how afraid I might be: look at me completely naked in your arms, what more do you want?

Tullie.

O Gods! If only you could grant me the power to do here what the veritable Pamphile could do! But alas! I think your power is limited, for I notice no change in my nature.

Octavie.

How's that, Tullie! Will Pamphile hold my tits that way? Will he kiss me so frequently as you do? & will he bite my lips, my neck, & my breasts like you do?

Tullie.

All these things, my little dear, are merely foreplay; there will be small forays that presage a much larger battle; & all these caresses can pass for bagatelles, & here you are comparing them to sovereign pleasure.

Octavie.

Ah! pull back, Tullie, you're placing your hand too far... below: ah! ah! you're pinching my buttocks; why are you touching me so forcibly there... what are you staring at?

Tullie.

I am contemplating, my love, with vivid pleasure, the field of Venus; I admire its beauty; it is clenched, it is tight, it is speckled with roses, & its charms will be heady enough to make the Gods visit earth.

Octavie.

I think you must be crazy, Tullie, to kiss me, to look at me, from top to bottom like that; I don't see anything in any part of my body that surpasses the beauty in your own; & you need only fix your gaze on yourself to satisfy your curiosity.

Tullie.

That would not be a modesty in me, but rather a stupidity, if I denied my being provisioned with some beauty: I am only nineteen years old; & having had only one child, I cannot have lost all the agreeableness that was formerly found in my person. That is why, Octavie, if you can take some sort of pleasure in me, go ahead, act freely, I will not oppose you.

Octavie.

Same deal for me; I grant you all that you desire: but I know that, given I'm such a young girl, you can't possibly take any enjoyment in me; & I also can't conceive of any pleasure I could derive from you, our being the same sex & all. That's not to say when I look at your face, that I don't imagine a garden planted with lilies & roses; forgive me for speaking like this, in these terms.

Tullie.

It is you, sauce box, who possesses a garden where Pamphile will cull flowers, & where he will enjoy fruits more delicious than the victual of the Gods.

Octavie.

What garden I have is the same as yours, as fruitful as my own. But what do you really mean by this "garden"? Where is it planted; what sorts of fruit are in it?

Tullie.

That smile of yours makes me realize your naughtiness: you pretend to be ignorant of something you know better about than I do.

Octavie.

You're referring to that part of my body you blocked the entrance to with your right hand, that you're massaging now with your fingers, & that you pinch & excite me by, while stroking it.

Tullie.

Yes, that is right; you have guessed correctly: but, being foolish, you have no idea what it is good for, & you are ignorant of its usage?

Octavie.

If I'd known about it outside of marriage, I'd be dishonest, & unworthy of your affection; but do me the kindness of instructing me: let's get back into bed; because seated as we are, all nude, we could catch a cold.

Tullie.

That is fine; but be attentive. The garden I spoke to you about, it is that part of your body located below your groin, in the middle of a small mount, covered with a little down: that fluffy cotton is a sure sign that a girl is in her maturity, & that the flower of her virginity is good to cull. There are many names for this part of the body; the madness of lovers makes them call it sometimes, *a Boat, a Field, a Ring,* &c., but the most common term is *a Cunt.* Admire, Octavie, the location of this part of the body (remove these sheets from you, you are so concerned with catching a cold). Do not think that it was placed between your thighs because of some mark of ignominy that it carries along with it, as our devout friends think; but only to make its use easier & more voluptuous. This small elevation you see there covered with a cottony moss is called the *Mons Veneris*; it is a kind of mountain, Octavie, that those who are fortunate enough to climb prefer to Parnassus, to Olympus, & to all the most famous mountains in antiquity.

Octavie.

Ah; how charming your lesson is, & how gladly I'd abandon to you the enjoyment of all parts of my body, which you seem to desire, to have in exchange a taste of the sweetness of your conversation!

Tullie.

Lie with me then, my dear girl, & quench with your kisses the intense love I feel for you now, do not refuse me anything, not to my eyes, not to my hands, all the pleasures that you can grant me: none of this will cause any harm, not to Pamphile, & not to you. But alas, how all my efforts are useless! How they are vain! & how miserable I am if I am unable to quench the fire than consumes me.

Octavie.

I make you the mistress of my body, & I grant to you the enjoyment of that part of it that you're massaging, if it can contribute to your contentment: let your will be your guide as you conduct your investigations.

Tullie.

You make me the mistress then of that path that leads to the supreme good: ah! I see the door to it; but alas! I cannot take advantage of the power you give me: I do not have the key to open it, nor the hammer to strike it with, nor any other instrument that could assist me in entering it. Ah, Octavie! Allow me to make an attempt.

Octavie.

Ah, God! What game are you trying to play by stretching yourself over me like this? What's this all about, – mouth to mouth, breast to breast, bellybutton to bellybutton! Tell me then what you intend by this pleasantry? Must I kiss you while you embrace me?

Tullie.

Yes, my little love, grant me that grace, & do not refuse a single one of my caresses, for they can only give you pleasure. Open your legs, & place them on mine: now that is good; you were so timely in obeying me, as I was prompt in commanding you.

Octavie.

Ah! ah! Tullie, how you press me; ah, Gods! What jolts! You have set me all on fire, you are killing me with these agitations: put those candles out at least, for I'm ashamed that the light might bear witness to what you're putting me through. Do you think, Tullie, I could endure this from anyone else but you?

Tullie.

My dear, dear Octavie, my love, love me with all you have got, & take... Ah, ah, ah! I cannot stand it, I am coming: ah, ah, ah, I am dying with pleasure!

Octavie.

Get off me, Tullie, you are crushing me with the weight of your body. What! You don't say anything? Have you lost the ability to speak?

Tullie.

Ah! it is over, my Goddess: I have been your husband, & you were my wife; never, (I swear to you) never have I felt such sensual pleasure, as what I just experienced now in your embrace.

Octavie.

Ah! may it please God that I should have so lovable a husband as you! That you would have a wife who cherished you; that she loved you, & that... Oh, God! I'm all wet! Where did that come from? I wasn't paying any attention: is that you, Tullie, who made me all wet? How's that possible?

Tullie.

Yes, it was me, my little dove, that did you this service; but what were your feelings during all this "playfulness"?

Octavie.

To tell you the truth, the pleasure I shared with you wasn't so great: I only felt some emotions; & some of the sparks of the fire that was burning inside you warmed me. But please, tell me, do other women have a similar love for their own sex, or is this illness particular to you?

Tullie.

Every woman, my dear child, burns with the same fire; & one would need be as cold as marble, & as hard as porphyry, to remain unmoved by the sight of something so lovable: for what more delightful thing is there in the world than a young girl, beautiful, soft, white, & clean just like you are?

Octavie.

Ah, cousin, I'm starting to feel a little sensation & a certain itch in that place that gives me pleasure; but I think it's nothing compared to the pleasure we feel from men when they sleep with us.

Tullie.

You are right, my little woman, & you will experience it tomorrow night with complete satisfaction; but much greater than if you received it from someone else than Pamphile.

Octavie.

And why's that, cousin? Aren't all men made in the same fashion?

Tullie.

No, poor innocent one: that is not it; it is because, outside of marriage, the pleasure we receive is always accompanied by fear & fright, & it is often followed by misgivings. In addition to pregnancy, birth & a thousand other inconveniences, which are the fruits born of our secret familiarities, expose us to strange accidents. But, on the other hand, in the pleasures of Hymen,[2] a satisfaction that is both bold & tranquil can be found, which is not found in any of the other kinds of pleasure; not to mention that marriage is a curtain that hides & covers the faults of our behavior during sex, given that we can divert ourselves without fear & without danger, as soon as we are fully dressed again. There are pleasures then for virgins, as well as for those outside of celibacy: they can discover in them a testing ground for the sensual pleasures that others feel; but much more pure because discord & jealousy almost never enter into them. Do not be surprised anymore then that a girl should conceive of love for another girl; as for myself, I burn with this passion night & day; & I would gladly trade Oronte's embraces for yours, although I love his a lot. You must not, then, my little saucy slut, think me indecent or dishonest; this humor of mine is not particular to me: French women, Italian women, Spanish women all cherish each other in the same way; & often, if modesty & shame did not restrain them, they would give public exhibitions of their passion, when they ran into each other.

Octavie.

Ah! I'm so charmed, cousin, by your discourse! I'd prefer my condition to those we esteem happier than ourselves, if only I was as wise as you.

---

[2]Hymen: marriage

Tullie.

Ah well, my Goddess, my love, my Venus, you are no less a virgin now than you were before; I did not want to do anything that would have robbed that beautiful flower that is reserved for Pamphile: he will continue to find the door to that garden shut, & he owes me some gratitude secretly, whether he knows it or not.

Octavie.

I think that Pamphile doesn't owe you much of anything; for if you hadn't opened it, it wasn't for lack of trying or desire, but for lack of strength rather.

Tullie.

It is clear to me that you have no idea what a *godemiche* is. The women of Milessi made them of leather, eight inches long, & proportionately thick. Aristophanes said that in his time almost all the women used them; today, among the Italians & the Spanish, they are still used often, & this instrument is one of the most precious objects in the toolbox of every Asian woman.

Octavie.

I haven't got the faintest idea what you're talking about, or what good it's for.

Tullie.

You will learn in time; but let us talk about something else now.

Third Academic Dialog

Players: Octavie, Tullie

Octavie.

Ah! ah! Ah! how you throw yourself at me! Ah! If the Gods had changed your sex, & had metamorphosed you into a man, what wouldn't be my lot now?

Tullie.

My dear love, Pamphile will act entirely the same; he will fill your mouth with kisses; he will suckle & suck on your two tits; in a word, he will cover your body with his, & he will shake you all the more pressingly, as he surpasses me in strength & vigor: his agitations will be so violent, that the bed you lie in will make a terrible racket, all the room will tremble, & the glass panes & the windows will break. I am not telling you anything I have not experienced myself; for the first night of my honeymoon when Oronte deflowered me, the efforts he made were so great, his movements so rude, & his agitations so surprising, that all those who were in rather distant rooms heard them quite clearly. Imagine for yourself, my dear, in what a state I found myself, me who carried away the victory, by the admission even of my adversary!

Octavie.

Ah! what'll become of me, if Pamphile's as vigorous as Oronte! If you had such trouble, although you're stronger & older than I am, ah! It's obvious that I'll succumb, & that I'll be unable to endure such rude attacks.

Tullie.

There is no point in trying to hide it from you; you will have to suffer a little, when Pamphile pierces you with his instrument: but also sweet feelings will follow that pain, pleasures & delightful sensations, that I cannot describe in words, & which will soon efface the least memory of past suffering.

Octavie.

Ah!, my dear Tullie, will I be mounted by a Knight as lovable as you? If that's the case, I won't envy at all Parnassus its Apollo, nor Mount Olympus its Jupiter. Ah! How happy Oronte must be to possess you in bed, & what a sweet life you lead. But what are you staring at, while opening my... Ah! You're extending the lips of my vagina a bit too widely; oh well! What do you see inside there?

Tullie.

What do I see? Ah! I see a flower, whose color & whose brightness surpass that of purple & scarlet. It is a treasure, the enjoyment & possession of which I would prefer to all the riches in the world.

Octavie.

Pull it out, I beg you, your lascivious finger, which you've put inside me; ah, ah! You push it in farther! you're hurting me; pull it out; again you push it in, – I beseech you.

Tullie.

Ah, how I pity you, precious seashell, a thousand times more suited for birthing Loves & the Graces than what Venus is said to have come out of! Ah! How happy Pamphile must be, & he must have been born under a favorable constellation, for the Gods have made him master of something that is at one & the same time so adorable & so sensually delightful!

Octavie.

Why're you saying that you have compassion for me, & that that part of my body makes you pity me? Must something bad happen to it or me?

Tullie.

It is the friendship that I have for you that makes me sensible to your sufferings, even before they materialize; I predict some pain & fatigue which you will suffer during Pamphile's first attacks. Ah, how the combat will be bloody! I imagine seeing with what cruelty that poor part of your body will be torn apart. Have you seen the weapon he wields?

Octavie.

No, I haven't, but I've felt it, & it seems to me to be like Hercules' club, as much because of its thickness as because of its prodigious length.

Tullie.

I know from Oronte that there is not a man in town better provisioned in that sense than Pamphile. Oronte has one that is eight inches long; but he says it is nothing compared to Pamphile's, & that Pamphile has a prick that is eleven inches long, & as thick as your arm (I am referring to your wrist).

Octavie.

Ah, Gods, what a monster! What, will he bury that entire prodigious machine into my belly? How'll I be able to endure such a thing? No, no, the very thought of it astonishes me & horrifies me, & my heart fails me at the mere suggestion of it. Eleven inches! Oh, great Gods!...

Tullie.

Do not lose heart, my child: although it is true that Pamphile's prick surpasses Oronte's in length, it must also cede to it in terms of thickness. Do you see my arm?

Octavie.

Most definitely, I see it.

Tullie.

Well, when his prick is hot, & when it is filled with passion for me, it is of the same thickness; & for all that, it is generally proportionate to its sheath.

Octavie.

I'm surprised he doesn't hurt you with all that, & that your vagina can so easily take it in. Is that even possible? You're going to need to satisfy my curiosity, & I'm going to need to see with my own eyes what I can't conceive of with my mind. Tullie, get on all fours on the bed, & turn your ass toward the light; spread your legs as much as you can, so that I can better consider the extent of that part of your body.

Tullie.

Alright, suit yourself; but be prepared to lose yourself down a path that is quite a bit larger than your own, & which has quite a few detours that are unknown to you. Am I in the right position? Is this how you want me?

Octavie.

Ah! God, how luxurious it is, how lubricated! Ah, I cannot look at your beautiful buns without being filled with lust; & I cannot stop myself from kissing them a thousand times.

Tullie.

Ah! how lascivious you are, little cousin! You are biting me! Stop this playfulness, & consider the length, the width, & the depth of that part of my body that you are investigating: good, open my labial folds there even wider; &, what do you see?

Octavie.

My God! What I see, I would never have believed it: I see that crack that Marcus Cortius[3] rode into, fully dressed for battle on his horse; I see a path where, I believe, Priapus himself could get lost in. Is it possible, Tullie, that my vagina should grow into something like yours without a metamorphosis on the part of the Gods?

Tullie.

Eh, well, are you happy now? & your curiosity, is it fully satisfied?

---

[3]Marcus Cortius: a mythical Roman soldier in the time of the Roman Republic who rode into a crack in the ground to appease the anger of the Gods.

Octavie.

Yes, I'm satisfied, & I've got such a good look at it, in that posture that you're in, that I think I'd like to know better what's hidden inside there, in that part of the body that makes us women. You still have to teach me, Tullie, something about the man's penis, & how one refers to it ordinarily.

Tullie.

I would like nothing better. You should know then that that part of a man's body is located in the same place as our own. It is commonly called a *cock*, (virile) *member*, *prick*, *dick*, *penis*, & by antonomasia, *nature*. There are a thousand other terms we use in our moments of passion to refer to it. Just know then that *prick*, *dick*, *cock*, or whatever else you want to call it, outside the love act, is soft & hangs down; & one might say that it is nothing but a picture, a foreshortening, compared to what it is in the heat of action, when it stands up, swells, elongates, but to an astonishing length, & becomes furious, which at first sight frightens us. In its attacks, when it takes possession of our virginity, it causes us a sensible & constant pain; but it is soon appeased by the excess of pleasure we receive a moment later.

Octavie.

The pleasure, I've no idea about that yet; the pain, I don't want to try; & as for the fear, – I've already experienced it.

Tullie.

Below that virile member, there is a well-stocked bag,

or scrotum, covered with little frizzy hairs, & which nature seems to have put there to conserve the heat of that part of the body, which must never be lacking. Now, in that scrotum there are two small globes that are the signs of virility: they are not of a regular roundness, but they are quite hard; & the harder they are, the more capable they are of giving pleasure. Vulgarly, one calls them *testicles*, or *balls*. There are some men in whom nature was so liberal with these treasures that they are equipped with three of them; like Agathocles, the Tyrant of Syracuse: & there is also a noble & illustrious family in Italy, all the descendants of whom have this same advantage. Admit it, Octavie, that the women of such athletes must be happy, & must enjoy quite a bit of good fortune, for there is nothing sweeter & more capable of appeasing our daily distress than when, by a prick's precipitous entry into the vagina, that smooth liquor, that sweet nectar, that precious elixir pours out in abundance from the porous veins of those small balls of flesh. That liqueur is called *seed*, *cum*, *sperm*, &c.; & of all the animals not one of them has it more in abundance than a man does; now imagine for yourself by what quantity of rain they are wetted, the women of those men who are so well endowed.

Octavie.

Well, maybe, Tullie, Pamphile also has three, & I've reason to believe it; for as I said, he wet me so profusely with his, that not only my thighs but all my belly up to my bellybutton were wet, not to mentioned my shirt & skirts.

Tullie.

That is not surprising; because it would be a humiliating thing for a young man like him, after making a sacrifice to Venus, or rather to beauty, not to spill on his victim that celestial dew in great abundance. That liquor is like the saliva from our vagina, but from the man; it is full of spirits, when it rushes out vehemently, & it is shot sometimes three feet away from the man. Imagine for yourself, Octavie, the excess of pleasure one feels, when after numerous shocks & frequent agitations, it finally discharges in the womb, & fills it with that divine ambrosia. Ah! It makes me wet just thinking about it, when we fall into ecstasy, we lose the usage of our senses, & our soul seems to abandon all its functions, in order to enjoy the moment with us, or rather in order to get drunk on the excess of that sensual pleasure. Ah! Octavie, there is no word or phrase that can express to you just how it is, the nature of that feeling of contentment. You will have to experience it for yourself.

Octavie.

I'll never grow tired, cousin, listening to you; & your conversation is so charming that I wished Oronte were absent more often, so that I can find the occasion to spend similar nights with you. What, you're yawning?!

Tullie.

Yes, my child, I am falling asleep, & I can no longer resist nodding off.

Octavie.

Let's continue our discussion; why're you going to sleep so early? Be so kind as to grant me that favor as

I caress you...

Tullie.

You have no idea what you need, crazy little girl: you have more need for sleep than I do; you should know that tomorrow night you will not be able to go to sleep, in the midst of Pamphile's passion & furious embraces: that is why you need to rest, in order to build your strength for sustaining, as a true daughter of Venus, all the attacks that he will make against you.

Octavie.

I'll do as you say, but more to please you than for any interest I might have in it; my health is, thank God, rather good, so as not to need all these cares & attentions. Sleep then, & I promise you I'll be quiet.

Tullie.

Give me a kiss, my love, before I close my eyes.

Octavie.

There, there's my mouth, my lips, & my entire body; all for you; do with it what you will.

Tullie.

Ah! kisses capable of making the Gods envious! Ah! How your embraces are filled with tenderness! How your touch is delicious! Allow me, my little whore, to sleep with you, like Mars reposes with Venus: that I might cover with one hand that so lovable part of your body, your vagina, that mount consecrated to love; & with the other hand I might touch your ass, & your so very white & tight buns. Now, that is nice, do not stir, not even a bit. And as soon as I wake up again, I promise you I will continue our conversations. Sleep, now, my little lover.

Octavie.

Sleep yourself: you're a strange babbler; you want rest, but you can't stop acting like a crazy woman, & playing around...

Fourth Academic Dialog

Players: Octavie, Tullie

Tullie.

How happy I am with my sleep just now! I slept profoundly for seven hours without interruption. And you, Octavie, how did you pass the night?

Octavie.

For me, it's about one hour now that I'm awake, & since waking I've felt extreme anxiety over a horrible vision that I had.

Tullie.

Let me hear it, I beg you.

Octavie.

I dreamt that Pamphile & me, we were strolling down a lane of trees in the fresh air, to protect ourselves from the sun, & he was making amorous complaints that were all the more agreeable as they came from a profound tenderness he had for me. He asked me for a kiss with extraordinary eagerness; I refused: but all my refusals only made him more obstinate & bold; & as he has infinitely more wit than me, he knew how to persuade me finally to let him have that kiss he so desired. But as you know, Tullie, in love, as one favor leads to another, he wasn't content with what I had granted him; he seized me with one hand, while slipping his other hand into my bosom. I put up a good fight, as best I could; & it was only by your assistance, Tullie, that I was able to break away from him. I had no sooner taken flight, than he pursued me with great speed; & at the moment when he was about to catch up, I turned my head. Ah, Tullie! If you knew what a monster I saw!

Tullie.

And what monster is that, cousin? Was it some ferocious wolf that had leapt up onto Pamphile's back? Or did his despair of reaching you make him run himself through with his sword?

Octavie.

No, nothing like that; God help him! Would that he might pierce me with his virile member than such an evil should happen to him. What I saw was this: listen, Tullie, you will be surprised; what I saw was Pamphile transformed into some ugly-looking Satyr, much like what painters represent on their canvas. His body was covered with fur; two goat horns stuck out of his forehead, rigid & pointy: as for his eyes, his nose, & the rest of his face, it looked normal. But that's not all: he was menacing me with his prick which was twice as long & two-times fatter than normal for the best-endowed of men; his thighs & his legs looked like a goat's; he rushed at me brusquely, kissed me, & with a total fury wanted to do it with me. What more can I say? That's the horrible vision that woke me up, & continues to make me shudder with fright. My dear Tullie, you who have so much erudition, you who know everything that can be learnt, can you explain to me so bizarre a dream?

Tullie.

Of course I can, & the interpretation is quite simple; but I will tell you at a different time & place, for it is not necessary that you know what it means right now.

Octavie.

Huh? Please, satisfy my curiosity, & don't leave me hanging any longer in the fears that are gripping me: I beg you, my little woman, or rather my little husband (since you have behaved in the same way toward me as a husband), I beg you, in the name of everything you hold most dear in this world, tell me.

Tullie.

Because you are so curious, I must satisfy you; there is no way I can refuse anything to the one I love. Understand then that this dream predicts the great pleasure that you will enjoy in youth, & that you will make love to a stranger; it also predicts that Pamphile will be blackened by this stain, which tarnishes today the reputation of a husband whose bed rights have been violated. In plain French, you will make him a cuckold.

Octavie.

Who me? I'd make a cuckold out of Pamphile! May God not even think about it!

Tullie.

I imagine it is not necessary to tell you who makes whom a cuckold; you must know that it is the wife, breaking the conjugal vow, who makes the husband a cuckold.

Octavie.

Of course I know that; but all the same, cousin, do you really believe I'm capable of making such a huge mistake? What, I would dishonor Pamphile like that? No, I'd rather die. Has it ever occurred to you to cheat on your Oronte? I could never believe it: I've too high an opinion of you & your integrity, & you will be so kind as to think the same of me.

Tullie.

Do not act so straitlaced, I am not telling you anything that should not happen to you. In the past, it was rather silly of people to believe that cuckoldry was an ignominy; but we have got past that today: for, at the end of the day, what is this great evil so many good people laugh at for good reason?

> *When one does not know about it, it means nothing;*
> *When one knows about it, it is not a big deal.*

Today, we have put that old error behind us then: all that remain are the sots who break their head over it; the better-informed among us will recognize that it is just an idea, pure & simple, nothing more; they do not say a word publicly though, & I think they are right; there is always more than enough for them: not to mention that since marriage is ordinarily the tomb of friendship, we have the right to look elsewhere for what might bring us pleasure. If men act like this everyday, even though they often have a beautiful wife waiting at home for them, a wife more beautiful than some other man's wife whom they take up with; – eh! Why should we not enjoy the same privileges they do? The union of wills makes the tightest marriage knot; if it comes undone, either by the vexation of humors, or by the great facility we have to grow quickly tired of what we have, the mutual obligation that we have to remain faithful – is there no end to it? (You understand this reasoning quite well.) Having become one of the completely liberated types of people, & our heart being unable to be without some sort of amusement, nature, which is wise in everything it does, allows it to seek some object that occupies its attention, & to grow attached to those that have some mutual sympathy.

Octavie.

Nevertheless I've seen some people who condemn these liberties you mention, like serious crimes.

Tullie.

I believe you; & it is true that civilian laws are contrary in this to those of nature; but it is only to avoid the disorder that could happen in society. Know then, Octavie, that the evil of cuckoldry that we are preached about ought not to frighten us, no more than that nice word "honor," which is not a real virtue, but a phantom & a pure chimera. Only, in our little love affairs, we should avoid to cause a scandal; it would be an extreme impudence to openly expose our husbands as cuckolds; one has to maintain appearances. By a false or true complaisance for the poor man, employ a bit of hypocrisy, make some grimaces at the right time & place, speak only rarely or not at all of the person we love, chose the appropriate hour for a tryst: this is the way to live happily in the bondage of marriage, concealing our heart's mystery; & to plant the horns of plenty on our husbands' forehead, without their knowing about it.

Octavie.

You surprise me, Tullie, by this admirable facility by which you have expressed yourself & spoken about these things: all your morals however will not lead me to do what you preach; I love Pamphile too much to pull the wool over his eyes like that.

Tullie.

Wait, wait a while until after you have lost your virginity, & I am sure that you will whistle a different tune, & that in some months' time your husband's caresses will grow insipid & less attractive to you. One grows weary of the same burden night & day, & a change is like a breath of fresh air; & there are very few women, if any, who do not seize the occasion when it offers itself.

Octavie.

I tell you again that nothing you say will persuade me, & that Pamphile can rest assured of my faithfulness; all that you say is fine & good, but it always has just enough in it to make me turn red in the face.

Tullie.

Ah! you sure are stubborn! Who, I ask you, can turn an insurmountable necessity into an opprobrium? If it is destiny that gives us so violent an inclination, what means do we have not to succumb? Minerva herself, & all the Vestal Virgins, could not resist; & you, you would have me believe... But let us get back to our dream; did you see anything else related to Pamphile?

Octavie.

Not a thing; & while you were sleeping like a log, I went back over it in my mind, all that you had recounted to me of the most secret mysteries of love.

Tullie.

I am delighted to have so good a student as you; I will make it so you pass with flying colors from out of my arms & into Pamphile's – as knowledgeable as needed to enjoy discriminately this pleasure. Let us continue our lesson: you already know that the penis must be inserted through this slit here, your twat, or pussy, which I have already described to you, & which is between your legs, – an arrow made of flesh will pierce you as far as your seventh rib.

Octavie.

Oh, my God! You're kidding me, Tullie; I hadn't the faintest... – how can that be?

Tullie.

However it might be, he will place it, that nerve of his, that thing that makes a man a man, into that part of your body that makes you a woman; your two sexes will romp around together, & the two of you will soon become one. That, in a nutshell, is how it works.

Octavie.

Ah! I can't tell you just how full of fear & desire I am! I wish to understand this mystery, & I expect you're going to teach me.

Tullie.

He will throw his arms around your neck to begin with, & he will press you so tightly to his body, – you are nude by the way – that it will be impossible for you to escape, even if you wanted to.

Octavie.

I beg you, my very dear Tullie, tell me how Oronte acted on the night of your honeymoon; for as far as Pamphile is concerned, you can tell me nothing for certain: tell me each kiss as it happened, in its own special way; some kisses more special than others I suppose, & I suspect that there is no general rule to any of this.

Tullie.

You are right, Octavie, I will satisfy you; & you will need to be cold as marble if you do not feel any emotion by the picture I will paint for you of our divertissements & the sex games Oronte & I acted out, when he took my virginity. Ah, Gods! What pleasures I enjoyed that night! The image I hold in my mind is too sweet for me to forget it: I will remember it forever. I grow wet thinking about it.

Octavie.

Begin then, Tullie; I'm more impatient than ever to hear you: you can speak without fear of being overheard; everyone in the house is sound asleep, all of nature reposes, silence reigns everywhere; in a word, everything is favorable for our pleasures & our games tonight.

Tullie.

After my mother had me get undressed & completely naked, she had me climb into bed; she put under the bedside table a bright-white linen towel; she then proceeded to kiss us, Oronte & me, & asked him to give me a kiss in her presence. This conduct by my mother completely confused me; after she retired, she closed the bedroom door behind her, & took the key with her into her room where there were lots of relatives, among whom my dear Angélique.

Octavie.

Is that the same Angélique you spoke to me about earlier, who was your best friend, & with whom you were on intimate terms?

Tullie.

Yes, that is her; if you knew her, you would be as charmed as I am by her beauty, her manners, & a certain something, I cannot put my finger on it, that wins over everyone's heart. Several months before I had my honeymoon, she was married to Lorance; he is a very nice young man in both body & mind. Angélique was therefore able to instruct me most precisely in the suffering I would endure after the first attacks were waged against my virginity; she taught me how I needed to act myself, what I needed to say, & she had not left out a thing as to what might make our pleasure greater; finally, I knew, in finest detail, all about how to ensure the perfect carnal union. Having been so well prepared, I waited for my adversary, with the resolution to fend for myself if he had more strength them me; I did not cede to him in anything in terms of courage, I only wished to have been free of a certain pudor, which got in the way of my being able at first to employ all my skill & dexterity on the field of battle.

Octavie.

I'm not at all surprised that you slept the entire night of your honeymoon with Oronte – nude: I know that my mother did the same thing on her honeymoon with my father.

Tullie.

One thing at a time: moderate a little that indiscreet ardor of yours to learn everything at once; just listen to me: when I am done, you will know everything there is to know; I will not forget one iota, & I will tell you all in the order it occurred. As soon as my mother had left the room, & Oronte realized he was completely alone with me in the place destined for our physical combat, he got out of his clothes quickly & appeared at the side of the bed in a flash, completely naked, when I was thinking he must have still been undressing.

Octavie.

It's quite clear he had a fire under his ass, & that he couldn't extinguish it without your help.

Tullie.

Ah! you sure like to joke! Do not interrupt me if you want to know everything you desire to learn. The room was bright as day – you could see everything. My mother had made a point of adding a large number of candles. I saw standing next to the bed a fine white, plump body; but having pretended to turn my eyes away for modesty, I noticed, further down, his prick, stiff as a pike; it was of a size to want to defend oneself against, & from time to time it lifted its head, as if it wished to greet me as a token of respect, or perhaps it was menacing me with the rude assault it was about to wage on me.

At first Oronte pulled all the covers off the bed (for it was the month of June when we were married), in this way exposing me completely naked before the cupidity of his eyes; I put my one hand over my breasts, & with the other hand I covered "that part," in order to conceal the two most precious places on my body, & to hide them from the light. But alas! I was not the mistress of these two locations for long; he took possession of them soon enough, by brushing my hands aside, & placing his own there instead. He looked at me with his amorous eyes full of passion; he kissed my mouth, my cheeks, my neck, my breasts, my tits, my belly, & performed all these acts so passionately & with such tenderness, that I was sensibly moved. After all these ceremonies of foreplay that were quite agreeable to me, he inserted his finger into my cunt as deep as it could go; & he did it (as he confessed to me himself in the heat of our embraces) to determine whether I was still a virgin: as far as a girl's virginity is concerned, the testimony of a finger is more certain than that of a penis. For be-

sides the fact that a penis in its fury is not capable of
making subtle discernments, because of its size it can
be inserted only up to its head, whereas a finger can
be easily inserted in its entirety.

Octavie.

Well, well; what a naughty little pilgrim!

Tullie.

All men are equally curious on this subject, & we
must forgive them the suspicions they have about us
women. But my how a new bride is joyful when her
man discovers her to be a virgin; & just what pleasure
a young groom finds when he plucks the flower that
is so rare to stumble upon these days! For when one is
a virgin as you are, & I was, there are evident signs in
the place where virginity resides; & what makes them
engage in their curious researches is that they know
that we lose our virginity not only by sex with other
men, but also by ourselves.

Octavie.

I hope you don't, Tullie, really mean what you're saying.

Tullie.

I will speak to you at another time about this matter;
all things have their proper place. Oronte having been
assured by the little entrance he made into my vagina,
& by the exact visit made by his finger, that I was as
he desired me, he jumped on me on the bed, embraced me; & by a thousand small caresses, & the
most passionate words you could ever imagine, he en-

deavored to engage me in... battle.

Octavie.

How's that! You who have such a pleasant & clever mind, you said nothing? Did you suddenly become mute? Were you turned to stone?

Tullie.

What would you have me do? I sighed in lieu of speaking; I pushed him back, one moment later I pulled him towards me, I fled & then I approached him: modesty, which was all over my face, stifled my most amorous desires, & at the same time stoked them; & this passion became more violent in me the more I wanted to put a stop to those furors. Oronte could by this time tell that I was completely hot in spite of myself: "Be brave, my dear Tullie," he said to me lovingly, "favor me, & don't get in the way of my enjoyment of a happiness, which depends entirely on you; open this little palace door that you have here, behind which sits the throne of the graces, laughter, & the most innocent play! My Goddess!" he said to me, smiling, "here is the key to the palace, take hold of it yourself;" but I refused. "What are you afraid of?" he continued; "if you are all mine, why refuse me these favors that are so rightly my due?" "Yes, Oronte," I said to him, "with all my heart I want to be all yours; but in order to be worthy of your esteem, do not make me, I entreat you, prostitute myself to all that filth you wish to drag me through; spare me my modesty: I have no doubt in the world that you love me; but it seems to me, with your furious insistence, that your passion has more of the character of hatred in it than integrity & steadfast love. My dear Oronte, – in the name of God! have some pity on me; will you not be moved by the tears you see me shedding?"

Octavie.

You were crying then, for real, cousin?

Tullie.

Yes, I shed several tears, but they had no effect on him. Just the opposite, he became more insistent: "If you love me," he said, "let's drop the modesty bit, I entreat you, it's really a bother; I'm surprised you even have any anymore, after having let a man all nude as myself see you all nude: you'll never have it again" he continued, "once you've shown me that you have no shame lying naked in front of me, & after you have performed in this conjugal bed everything I think necessary for our shared pleasure. You ought to know the power I have over you legally, on account of the law of marriage, which is why you can't oppose anything." During all this talk, his penis was furious, & it was beating its head against my two thighs, as if it were enraged for what we could not give it.

Octavie.

Ah! my poor Tullie, how I pity you! The wounds that you were about to receive make me shudder with fear for you!

Tullie.

You make fun of everything; now, listen carefully, if you are smart, to the most serious thing in the world.

Octavie.

"Ah! ah! Ah!..." Well, I'm listening, go on, & don't get upset.

Tullie.

Without further ado, he forces my legs open with one of his legs, & discovers the path he wants to take: he immediately mounts me by lying on top of me with the full extent of his body. What could I do? I was completely surprised to find myself pinned down by so heavy & massive a weight; he took his instrument in hand, as if to stop its sudden movements, & positioning the tip of it right at the lips of my vagina, he laid into me with all he possessed: but he could not proceed; for the pass was too narrow to let pass so fierce an enemy at first. On the first & second attempts, he gained not one inch of terrain; on the third & fourth attempts, I felt that the spirits of Priapus coming to his rescue (you know, Octavie, what I mean by "spirits of Priapus" – that precious pre-ejaculate fluid that nature has endowed us with & has consecrated to the generation of the species & sensual delight); & then, as if the floodgates holding back this divine liquor had been thrown open, there was a kind of deluge everywhere, all over my body. This was but a skirmish, & not a real battle; I was suffering however with a burning pain inside that part of my body, my nether parts, as a result of the violent & reiterated efforts that my adversary had made in his attempt to take possession of the place.

Octavie.

Were you able to stifle your cries?

Tullie.

Sounds easy! I cried as if someone had just torn the skin off my back. I grew calmer however a little later, because Oronte was complaisant enough to lighten up & make some small talk, for fear of making me cry even more: he grew playful, & came up with this: he placed his penis in such a way that the head was nearly touching my navel; & all that area in between it & my breasts was inundated with semen. I then took the linen towel that was under the table beside the bed, as my mother had instructed me to do, & I first cleaned his prick, then dried the parts of my body that were still wet. During this time, he was devouring me with kisses; & like a man who returns from ecstasy, he could only sigh, but not utter a single word.

Octavie.

Ah! the poor child, she was having such a tough time of it!

Tullie.

After these first attempts, he rested for a moment: "May I be struck dead instantly," he said to me, "if I don't love you more than my eyes, more than my life! Is there anything more beautiful in the world to gaze on than you? Are you a Goddess or a mortal? Ah, Gods! What beautiful breasts! I can't imagine Venus' tits being any firmer, rounder, & more perfectly situated at the right distance from the each other." He was fondling them as he spoke, he could not satisfy himself by just looking at them; he kissed them, he sucked them with the extremity of his lips, & bit gently at the nipple which is one of their principal charms.

I have to confess to you, Octavie, that these little sex games he came up with pleased me infinitely, & made me want to go at it a second time. He then put one of his hands between my thighs & played around with my downy pubic hair; he pressed together the lips of my little vagina, one against the other; afterwards he opened it up & put the fingers of his hand inside, one finger after the other. "Here's what I'd like to do," he said:

> *"I do so love these sex games:*
> *I wish each finger were a penis...*
> *You'd be much more content;*
> *Not to mention these penises*
> *Would never grow tired*
> *Of paying you their rent."*

I curchied (as best one can in bed) & said: "I am much obliged to you, kind sir, for all your best wishes; this makes me wonder though. If one penis causes me so much pain, what would ten do? Assuredly you would kill me before I could get out of this bed. Nature is very wise to make men come so quickly; be content with what you have, friend, & do not make a criminal offense out of your lubricity by so extravagant a desire." Oronte heard me with pleasure, & laughed out loud with all his heart at my simplicity. Try as I might to reason with him & act upset, he held his hand all the while on my clit; & brandishing at me with his other hand his furious war hammer, he told me to take it. I refused at first; but having grown a bit more bold, I obeyed him. Ah, what a monster! Will you believe it, Octavie? I could barely hold it in my hand; & I felt gripped with horror on seeing it so rude, hard, & hot. "That is the weapon," he continued, "that I will use to split you down the middle, & I will break those doors down with it & plunder that virginity of yours that seems so inaccessible. Courage, my little Nymph, my Goddess; it's with the hope that I'll come away the victor that your mother gave you to me; when she returns to offer us her felicitations, what would she say if she found you just as much a virgin as before? She'll treat me like a coward & an imbecile, & she won't want me for her son-in-law, my being unable to exercise on you the function of a husband." "Ah, my dear Oronte!" I said to him in reply, "you are going to kill me then, infallibly, if you expect to insert by force so large & furious a penis into my belly!" But he was deaf to my words; he mounted his beast once again, & I led with my hand the frothy steed as far as the doors of the stable. This time, he lifted up one of my thighs; & under my auspices, he pushed & pushed again forcibly, with his cock: I endured patiently these first attacks; but in a moment he became so furious, that after having pushed more vigorously than before, he succeed in inserting it by about two inches.

Octavie.

Did it hurt?

Tullie.

I felt an incredible amount of pain. "You are killing me, Oronte," I told him. I was crying in a pitiable voice, or rather, those were not cries so much as howls. Angrily, I yanked his prick out of my vagina with my hand; but then he got upset, & made a rude comment, to the point that he treated me insolently for having been so bold. I was forced then to appease him, to put it back in its place, where it was not long before... out came a rain of milk and honey that reduced a little the pain he had been causing me. His penis grew soft then & weary, after that last attack, & he needed to call a brief timeout.

Octavie.

Tell me, Tullie, had that rain got inside you at all?

Tullie.

No, my dear, only a small drop; it was only the edges & extremities that were dampened by that sweet liquor. Oronte however was complaining loudly now: "If you loved me, Tullie," he said, "you wouldn't refuse me the veritable fruits of your love, treating me like some miserable beggar: I'm dying for you." "I love you too," I responded, "& with the tenderest love in the world: miserable as I am! Is it your intent to make a butcher's shop of this bed? Keep in mind that I am quite young yet, & that I have a body that is extremely delicate." "Don't you know," he said, "that that part of your body does not belong to you, but to me? How can you not know this, you who have such fine acquaintances? Why dispute with me then the enjoyment & the possession of a thing that is mine, & that so rightly is my due?" "Ah! Oronte," I said to him, "if you knew how cruel you are acting, & the pain you make me suffer, how excruciating it is, —

you would show some pity to your Tullie, assuming you loved her." "This pain," he responded, "can only be glorious for you; & the more it smarts, the more honest you appear, not to mention that it won't last long, & that it ought to be followed by a pleasure that is endless. Do you know," he added, "that you have made a grave mistake by making me spill this divine semen on the outside? There is no greater crime: you have taken away from me the advantage of becoming a father; you have murdered my children & your own, before they were born; you have thrown away the soul they didn't have; see how criminal your impatience has been!"

"My dear husband," I said to him, "I do not wish to argue with you about that; I admit that I am culpable; forgive me: I will try to be more submissive; I will suffer, with constancy, all the pain you wish to inflict on me; & to add to your pleasure, I will act as best I can. 'O Goddess!'" I said, more for myself than for him, "You who presides over Hymen, favor me; inspire in me more amorous feelings, & make me move more in sync with the inclinations of my dear Oronte, & I will obey you will blindly." He was satisfied with this submissiveness; he kissed me many times, touched me, squeezed me & fondled me all over: all these little games were normally the horn blowers of renewed combat to me. "Let's go," he said to me, "be brave, do what you've promised to do. Look how your enemy has become redoubtable in so small amount of time! He seems, at first glance, to want to bathe everything in fire & blood: but however furious he might appear, you can easily conquer him; wait for him at the gate only, without yielding ground; & during combat, invoke devoutly the God of love battles. There," he continued, "lie down, & do what I tell you, if you want me to be your husband. Lift your legs as high as you can, & lower your feet when I'm on top of you: very good; now, hold me with all your strength, so that I can't escape."

Octavie.

You kept your word, no doubt?

Tullie.

Yes, I did as he told me to with my legs, & I held him so tightly, that one might have said I wanted to fuse myself to him. He began by kissing my eyes, & opened my pussy with his fingers, which he tried to enter. He placed his war machine at its entrance, & made such a show of strength that he was able to go farther in than he had before. Seriously, Octavie, I thought he was going to shred me to pieces; my pain was so great that not only could I not hold back the tears, but I was also unable to prevent myself from crying out loud, at the top of my lungs. Oronte then took some pity on me, he stopped in the middle of his adventure: "I'm going to stop for a moment," he said; "be brave though, because you don't have much more to suffer; I've made it more than half way through; see for yourself." The danger I felt I was in made me bring my hand there, & I found that he was telling the truth; but the part of his penis that still remained out-side was fat & more nervous: I was speechless; & af-ter having pushed once or twice, he entered further into the wound. "Ah, how miserable I am!" I said, "you are killing me; stop my dear Oronte, moderate a bit these cruel blows." For all that, in spite of my suffering, I held on to him tightly with my arms, & I continued to hold my legs in the air so as to help him by this position to finish up quickly the grand affair. Finally, after the fourth jolt, having mustered all his strength, he made Priapus glorious & triumphant, & it entered in its entirety into a place that had been so well defended. The bed, which was the battlefield, trembled, & the noise it made was so loud that it made all my relatives, who were in the adjoining room, imagine that it had been broken to pieces. I screamed louder than ever, & I begged Oronte to pull out from the wound the arrow he had pierced me with: it went as far in as my entrails. "It's at this time," he said to me calmly, "that I can say that, from the very pure virgin that you were, you have now become a very chaste woman: you have nothing more to fear; the road to pleasure is clear; it's open to you & me; I've paved the way: all your suffering is behind you now: & I'm going to sprinkle that water of Venus all over the floor inside, & I will give you a kiss as a signal before I do." As soon as he said this, he kissed me, & at the same moment I felt myself all wet inside, as far as my entrails, with a warm & viscous blood. All the pleasure that I felt then was but a light tickling sensation. Not so with Oronte; the continuous kisses he gave me, his touches, his sweet words intermixed with amorous sighs, his eyes looking half alive, half dead, testified more than enough that his joy was infinite.

Although he had discharged his duty as a valiant man, he was not given to blathering. But he did say this to me, pleasingly: "I want to repay you for all the damage I've caused you, & I want to take advantage of my privilege as the victor." "What! Oronte," I said to him, "you are still not satisfied? Tell me: what are the rights of a victor? I will accept the laws you want to impose on me, be it as a slave, or as a free woman." "When a man has become master of a place," he responded, "which has cost him so much sweat & blood, as the taking of yours has cost me, he can remain there as long as he likes; there is nothing you can do that can force him to leave: that's all there is, Tullie, – the most sacred rights of a victorious penis; & I want you to admit to your defeat, & I want your pussy to admit that she's completely destroyed, completely broken apart, as acknowledgement to her sovereign lord. But, prepare yourself for a new assault: as of now, you are at the end of your suffering, & I want you to confess when I'm done with you that there is no sensual delight on earth more solid & more sweet among mortals than that between Venus & Mars. To make you more sensible of this, I will teach you what you must do; while I'm pushing down, you push up, as vigorously as you can: it will not be difficult for you who are young & robust." I obeyed him; I did my duty so well that my buns were more active than his were. Oronte, on seeing that I was so knowledgeable & skillful in the act, said: "Courage, push, push, harder, harder, what an Amazon! My soul, my little sweetmeat, my Venus, how pleasurable you make me feel! There is no mortal happier than me! Ah! Gods! I don't envy your felicity; what I enjoy now is one thousand times more pure & more solid than yours: ah, ah, ah, Tullie, my dear Tullie, I'm dying!" "And me, Oronte," I said, "I feel, ah!... I feel... as though... I cannot say what."

Octavie.

You're killing me, Tullie, by your discourse; I'm dying... in expectation of so great a pleasure.

Tullie.

While we were so tightly coupled together, I felt that liquor flow, which, by its stimulation, made me want to come at the same time, which I did. I felt a burning, tingling sensation all over my body, a furious heat, & having no more modesty in view, I pressed my enemy, I fatigued him with my sallies: one would have said, in view of the mobility of my buns, that my butt was so full of quicksilver that nothing could fix it. Finally, we were so happy this time around that the two ejaculations occurred at the same moment; this was accompanied by so much bravery on both sides that if Venus had been our witness I believe she would have been hard pressed to decide whom to award the laurel wreath to. We had barely begun to breathe again, Oronte & I, when we heard the door to the room open; my mother & Angélique entered quickly & locked the bolt behind them.

Octavie.

Clearly, on entering, they could see that Oronte had already put the bolt inside you, right?

Tullie.

Keep laughing, you crazy girl; you will not be laughing so hard when you feel the assaults made against your maidenhead in a few hours.

Octavie.

All things in good time: go on with your story.

Tullie.

At first I took the covers that Oronte had pulled back to the foot of the bed and I covered his nudity with them, & my own: for I was ashamed of that gear being seen by my mother; I was not so concerned about Angélique, for we had known each other just like you & I do. My mother gave me a hug, then addressed herself to Oronte: "My son," she said, "my how you have fought bravely! You are a hero; my daughter's cries are irrevocable testimony of her defeat: I congratulate you on your victory; if you hadn't come away the victor, Tullie would have been a widow, although married. Angélique then threw her arms around me & gave me a thousand kisses, with tears in her eyes. "Ah! My poor child," she said to me in a low voice, "Oronte has treated you so badly!" She spoke in earnest. "Every time I heard your voice screaming so loudly, I cursed him with all my heart; but tell me, how are you doing?" "Quite well," I said to her; "and finally, after so much labor & cruel suffering, I have tasted that great pleasure that is the ultimate happiness in life." "Are you a woman?" she added. "Yes, I am. You are so sweet to ask; & when I go over again in my mind the great possession gained just now by the loss of my virginity, I admit that the richest treasures are no comparison: I am already so accustomed to it that I would rather give up eating & drinking than these agreeable pastimes." "Excellent," she said to me: "you speak like a Sibyl,[4] & any girl that does not get a taste of Venus' sensual delights cannot really enjoy her life the way she should. Given we all have a violent penchant, one is often advised to moderate those innocent, natural impulses by chimerical ideas of honor; one might even want religion to have a say in the matter: all the sots who say so are afraid of it; but the sages do not believe a word of it; what they do do, however, is to avoid letting the outside look in, & hide behind appearances, in order to accommodate the century's ignorance..." She would have continued her moralizing, if Oronte had not drawn near. Angélique greeted him & congratulated him, by way of compliment, for what he had happily succeeded in doing, with a maidenhead that would have given Jupiter even a run for his money.

Did you know that Angélique has a great wit, & that she says things with an air that pleases everyone in the world who hears her? My mother poured a big glass of hippocras for Oronte: "Drink it, my son," she said to him, "to fortify you & repair the strength you have expended; if you take my advice, you will repose for a bit; you have earned enough glory for one night." She made me eat three candied walnuts, & whispered quietly in my ear to try & obtain from Oronte three hours of respite, because I needed some sleep. While she turned to return to her company, Oronte called Angélique & asked her to stay a moment to witness his valor: as soon as she looked at him, he leapt on me brusquely, & administered such vigorous jolts that one would have thought the bed

---

[4] Sibyl: a prophetess.

was threatened with imminent ruin, it trembled so much. My mother & Angélique burst out laughing. And far from defending me, they left me completely alone, to fend for myself against Oronte's furor. His lap around the field this time was a bit longer than ordinary; but also his semen penetrated more deeply into my womb, where I felt a light stimulation, that caused me a kind of lethargy in all my senses. When the business was over, our knight abandoned his post, & exited completely attenuated, with head lowered.

Octavie.

No doubt, in that humiliating posture, he asked your pardon for the blood he'd made you lose?

Tullie.

I wanted to dry him with the linen as before. "No need," he said to me; "it's as dry as if it hadn't swum in the pond of voluptuousness." Then he placed his hand on my nether part; & having pushed a finger deep into it, he found that my womb was not at all wet. "May the Gods look kindly upon us!" he exclaimed, "I have no doubt that with this last attack the fruit of our love will grow in your belly, my dear Tullie. That's enough for now, sweetheart; rest up a bit, until I challenge you to new combats." How tired I was; sleep quickly took possession of all my senses; I slept for three hours, during which Oronte did not close his eyes. He kissed me from time to time, & watched me the whole while; I slept so profoundly that I never woke up: he gently pulled up the sheets & the bedcover (I was sleeping on my back); & having gently spread my legs, he looked at the sensuous ring where he had run three laps. He admired the beauty of my body; & in this agreeable contemplation, enflamed by so charming a sight, he made his entry into that place that he had so well visited. On the arrival of so lovable a guest, I opened my eyes to receive him. "What a joy," he exclaimed, "you live, my Goddess! I was afraid I might have had the same experience as Periander, the Tyrant of Syracuse, who fondled a dead woman." "Be assured, I will make you see," I told him, "that I am very much alive." "Well, my love, do as you say then; you cannot," he responded, "give me any greater sign of your love."

Octavie.

What'd you do to show him that you were alive? I can probably guess.

Tullie.

Well! Say it then, what do you think?

Octavie.

I think that you moved your behind as fast as you could.

Tullie.

You have hit the nail on the head, Octavie; that is it. Being on my back, & feeling myself pinned down, when Oronte pushed down, I pushed up, with an extraordinary vigor. While this cadence lasted, we were belly to belly, chest to chest; finally, we were so closely bound together one against the other that if Oronte's body had been covered with semen from head to foot, I would have been as well – to the last drop.

Octavie.

This battle lasted long?

Tullie.

Alas! Only an instant; because if we measure the pleasure by its duration, we would find that it is over too quickly, even if it lasted a century. It seems to me that nature made a big mistake when creating us: its masterpiece would have been even more accomplished if it had placed in our vagina a pool full of semen that the man's penis could swim in, & that his member should have been made in the likeness of a fountain, & a boisterous source of that same liquid.

Octavie.

You who are so wise, cousin, tell me why this pleasure is so brief.

Tullie

It is not easy to find an answer to that; this difficulty baffled all antiquity, & not a single person had the audacity to try & settle the matter: but I love you too much, my sweetheart, to refuse you; here is what I think.

To unravel this question, you must know that the philosophers were not all in agreement as to the seat of the soul: Hippocrates put it at the ventricle in the brain. Zeno & the Stoics at the head & at the heart; Empedocles put it in the blood; as did Moses: which is why that sage legislator forbade the Jews from drinking the blood of animals. Galen believed that each part of the body had its own soul; Aristotle, that it was spread throughout the body; & me (may it not displease all these great men) I think that the true seat of the soul is in the testicles of men & in the ovaries of women. According to this opinion, it is easy to answer the question that you put to me touching on the brevity of venereal pleasure; for as I have just explained to you, if semen is the seat of the soul (as it clearly is) *ergo* each drop that leaves it is a part of the whole: to the effect that nature was very wise to moderate its ejaculation, lest that by abandoning the whole matter to our immoderate pleasure, we would evacuate the entire wad, which, being the soul, would bring the entire human race down with it. By way of proof, we see men everyday who do not wish to moderate their pleasure, & who repent of it, & that their lubricity costs them their life, by the exhaustion of their vital spirits that are expended during battles repeated too often. It is true that women run the same risks, because...

Octavie.

That's enough, Tullie; what you're saying now is too erudite for me: I'd be obliged if you continued with your story instead, which I imprudently interrupted by my curiosity.

Tullie.

Where was I? If I am not mistaken, it was when Oronte wakened me with his penis. The leisure that he had had during the three hours that I slept, to contemplate me, had so heated his imagination, that his instrument was full & frothy: I felt it rummaging around inside me, inside my entrails, & I wiggled so much, that the whole business came to an end in no time, for Oronte with this fourth romp had paid out the ordinary tribute of semen so that, after it was mixed together with mine, we were left speechless.

Octavie.

Tell me, please, my dear, did he cause you any harm with this fourth attack? I'm curious to know, because I'm burning with desire to enjoy the same pleasures soon, which you represent to me as being so great, & also because I'm afraid of the pain that'll precede them; consequently my heart wavers between hope & fear.

Tullie.

Ah, how silly you are to be frightened for so little! Whatever pain there might be, the pleasure is infinitely greater.

Octavie.

I believe you, cousin; because merely by hearing you speak, I feel an arousal & a strange tickling sensation in this part.

Tullie.

So much the better, so much the better, it is a good sign; you can, while waiting, without too much mystery, satisfy your itch if it becomes too strong. No, no, let me do it, I understand perfectly...

Octavie.

This itching sensation I feel is on account of your talk; your expressions are so vivid & natural, you represent things as if they were lying right before my eyes, as if I were feeling them myself. But what are you doing, Tullie? Ah, pull your adulterous finger out of there, you're exciting me! Finish telling your story, please! how you passed the rest of the night with your little husband.

Tullie.

Oronte fell asleep for several hours; as for me, I did not even close my eyes, although I had such a desire for rest: but the flames in me were still burning, & I was struck with the idea of opening the window that looks out over the garden. I got out of bed, completely naked, & I opened the window without waking Oronte; I snuffed out the flames, for day was breaking; & because I had a desire to piss, I took hold of the chamberpot; but as the urine was tinkling, it caused such a sharp & biting pain in me, that I could hardly stand it. The groans I let out woke Oronte up; he stared at me & said: "Where does it hurt, sweetheart?" I immediately got off the chamberpot, although I had not finished. "I thought you were sleeping," I said to him; "I hope I have not offended you by the sight of some dishonorable act." "Yes, that's really too bad," he said, "that I saw you pissing; but you should know that a thing ceases to be dishonorable as soon as it's necessary. Fucking, drinking, eating, sleeping, pissing, &c., are actions one cannot do without – without ceasing to live, & by consequence they contain no filthy image. I sat down on the edge of the bed & remained quiet, after having dried myself completely. Oronte grabbed me immediately between his arms & his legs; he kissed me, & slapped me gently on the butt, first with one hand, then the other. He asked me to take his prick, in order to excite it to a new combat; I obeyed him; & in short order, I saw it growing larger, visibly, right under my nose (the hand of a beautiful girl has a marvelous virtue to make this happen). "I want to ride you now," he said, "in a new way; put your left leg on my right one." I did it: he pushed dreadfully hard, but he could not enter because our positions made access difficult. He made me raise my left leg even higher; but for all that, he could only enter halfway; when, weary of this position that was uncomfortable for me, I threw one leg here, & one leg there... & presto, before you know it I was on top: I confess that it was glorious to see my adversary beneath me, & I goaded him on so well that we arrived in safe harbor. Oronte confessed that he had never tasted so delicious a pleasure in his life.

Octavie.

Apparently you didn't feel any pain?

Tullie.

No, because by moving my legs, I got rid of the rest of my pain, besides which the path had already been beaten. During this activity, I tickled his scrotum lightly, I squeezed his two balls with my fingers, I stimulated him to such a degree by this playful act, that they spilled with profusion that divine liquor which they are the depositaries of.

Even though I had come, I was not ready to

abandon the field so soon, & as all my pudor was completely vanished by now, what with my being on top, I kissed Oronte's eyes, his mouth, everywhere; I nibbled his lips, his cheeks; I fondled him all over his body with my hand; I pinched his butt; I tickled him; &, finally, I paid him back with interest for all the fondling he had lavished on me in our first embraces. My mother promised that she would come visit us again in the morning; we heard her approaching; "Come in whoever you are!" said Oronte; "I promised you seven laps," he said to me, "and I still owe you one, let's do it now, so that I might keep my word." As soon as he heard my mother approaching the room, & just as she was inserting the key into the lock, he climbed on me: "Here you go," he said, "divine Tullie, behold the key that I will use to open your cabinet;" at that moment he entered me & shook me so violently that when my mother entered, she was completely surprised to hear the bed shaking so loudly: I pretended to sigh for shame, & to get upset with her. "What do I see here," she said, "daughter? Was last night not long enough for your debates? My faith, you're really abandoning yourself to the joys of sex." "I beg your pardon, mother," I said to her, "I am really upset that you have surprised me in the middle of this turpitude." But Oronte jolted me vigorously, as if my mother's presence had encouraged him. "Just listen," she told me, "to your husband, & have no shame in fulfilling your duty as a wife; I will leave you two now, to let you finish in peace." As soon as she left the room, Oronte, warmed up with the passion for combat, asked me to do my duty. I understood exactly what he meant: that is why as he advanced, I fought back, as if I had wanted to throw him up at the ceiling of the bed. He praised my courage, & was charmed by the mobility of my buns; I told him he should praise me instead for the love I had for him, which made me forget myself, abandoning myself in acts that were so improper for a young woman. But as soon as I felt the moment of pleasure approaching, it felt as though all the veins in my womb had opened: "Do it quickly, Oronte, I cannot last, I am dying, ah! ah! ah!..." The poor boy went as fast & as hard as he possibly could to relieve me; but no matter how he moved his cheeks, not a single drop of semen came out of his pipe: one could say that his source had dried up. He kissed me tenderly, & entreated me to help him in this great effort: I succeeded so well that I got him to ejaculate finally; but he did it a long time after me. Then after resting for a long time in my arms without saying a word, contemplative, he got up out of bed, called his valets, & got dressed; first he gave me a kiss, asking me forgiveness for having shown such laxity with me: then this is what he said to me: "I'm ashamed, my dear, to have run so few laps around so beautiful a field." While he was bantering like this, my mother returned with Angélique; they brought in two large bowls of consommé; my mother gave one to Oronte, & Angélique gave the other one to me, which I gulped downed immediately. Oronte, in order to appear more valiant, said he did not have need of it; nonetheless, he drank it like me, without causing much of a fuss.

Octavie.

I imagine, Tullie, you have painted a faithful picture

of what I might expect, in your discourse just now: which consoles me, as much to say if Pamphile causes me as much suffering as Oronte caused you, I'll also experience the same pleasures you did, & maybe even they might seem sweeter; because my vagina is smaller & tighter than yours, & Pamphile's penis is three inches longer than your husband's, – it'll give me more pleasure, as he'll penetrate me more deeply.

Tullie.

I only hope, my dear girl, & I say this to you as a friend, that Pamphile performs his duty as well as Oronte acquitted himself of his. But it is time for us to get out of bed now; I think that if you had slept on Parnassus, you would have received no better instruction, & I hope that with the lessons I have just given you, you will defend yourself against Pamphile's attacks as dexterously as anyone your age.

Octavie.

I'm infinitely obliged to you, cousin; I know, I believe, enough now: provided that Venus & her son favor me, I've such good hope of my skill & my courage that I hope I won't let out a single cry, nor shed a tear, in the fiercest heat of battle.

Tullie.

Oh, God no! I must warn you against doing that, my poor child! Such constancy could take a negative turn for you, & would make Pamphile suspect something that is not to your advantage. Nothing gives a husband more joy, on the first night of marriage, than when his bride bears witness by her tears to just how much suffering he is causing her: he takes those wails & those sighs for the last gasps of a dying virginity. Reflect carefully then on what you have to do, & remember that I speak to you as a friend.

Octavie.

You're right, cousin; thank you *so* much: I'll cry so loudly that Pamphile won't have any doubt in his mind as to my virginity. Give me a kiss, kind Tullie, before you climb out of bed.

Fifth Academic Dialog

Players: Octavie, Tullie

Tullie.

Ah! My very dear cousin, come in, come in: I just arrived yesterday from the country, where I left Oronte, & I was so impatient to see you again. Well, what is it! What does you heart tell you? But how is it you arrive so late?

Octavie.

I come, cousin, with the intention of spending the night with you; I have to confess that the last two weeks, in which we haven't seen each other, have seemed like a century to me, even though I passed them amidst sensual pleasure. I found in Pamphile's embraces all the sweetness that you had led me to expect: he did his duty & acquitted himself as a galant man; he waged battle on the plain of love with such vigor, that he was obliged to retire to the country to find some rest, & relax from those amorous jousts. In a word, my very dear cousin, I have reason to be satisfied.

Tullie.

I am delighted to hear that, my little cutie-pie; & I am even more delighted to know that we will sleep together this evening, & that we can speak freely about our love makings: it is late: what are we waiting for: let us hop into bed so that we can embrace, & so that I can hear what happened between Pamphile & you. Come, let us sleep together then.

Octavie.

I'm so looking forward to it, with all my heart, my very dear cousin, & I hope I can infuse into your body the same torrents of voluptuousness that mine was made wet with; I would that your body could be as sensible to these pleasures as your mind will be to the story I'm about to tell you. Look at me: I'm already undressed.

Tullie.

Me too; but you need to take off your shirt, there is nothing like lying in bed flesh against flesh.

Octavie.

Ah, you're naughty! you're taking my chemise off me; let me take it off myself. Ah, Gods! how you paw me & throw yourself at me, one leg here, & one leg there! What's gotten into you? Let's climb into bed then.

Tullie.

Okay, here we are, my little lover; now kiss me, tenderly.

Octavie.

As many kisses as you like; but please, remove your adulterous hand from there... you don't want to sully a young married woman like that, do you?

Tullie.

Are you crazy! What have you got to fear from me?

Take away your hand: let me enjoy the pleasure I wish; besides, I was with you before Pamphile; & I left those candles lit on purpose, so that my eyes might have the pleasure of seeing you, just as my other senses enjoy tasting you, feeling you, touching you....

Octavie.

But, Tullie, shouldn't the laws of friendship give way to those of conjugal love? If I let you have your way with my body now, as you have done before, won't I offend my husband?

Tullie.

Are you really capable of so foolish a thought? How can that be possible! you have nothing to reproach me for: ah, ah, ah!

Octavie.

What?! why are you laughing?

Tullie.

Ah, Gods! what a metamorphosis! that little slit that used to be the seat of your virginity has been transformed into something else, of prodigious extent. Ah! bounty of Venus! what an opening! Spread your legs a little.

Octavie.

Oh, well. How do you want it, bad girl; I'll obey.

Tullie.

Ah! how the Cunt of a woman is different from that of a virgin! Ah! ah! Gods! What an opening! I think I could even slip my entire hand in there.

Octavie.

Eh, eh, eh, you're setting me all afire. I can't hold out much longer, if you don't pull out your hand. Do you want me to commit an adultery in your hands, me who would rather die than violate the oath I made?

Tullie.

We will see soon enough if these feelings of yours last. However, let me admire this prodigious change in you: no, I believe that of all men only Pamphile could fill this gap. You are much wider than me now; even though I have already had a child, & I have often diverted myself with many others: I suspect also that it will not make you unreceptive to pleasure.

Octavie.

What difference does that make, provided that Pamphile is content, & that his shaft is proportionate to my sheath: because it's for him alone that this road was made for traveling, & for no others. What is surprising however is that with all this width, with all this breadth, the last time he rode me he complained that I'm pinching him everywhere, that it's as tight as if I had been squeezing him with my hands. In the end, he admitted that the pleasure he felt could not be any greater.

Tullie.

And you, what did you say?

Octavie.

I didn't say anything, but I egged him on by a thousand tender kisses; I relieved him by my jolts, & by the small movements of my buttocks, which I did from time to time.

Tullie.

Ah! if you want to, my dear, – tell me everything that happened while you were making love, from beginning to end; it will give me such satisfaction to hear!

Octavie.

I'd like nothing better, Tullie, given that I cannot think about these sweet pastimes without feeling their pleasures all over again. You know then that before I got out of bed with you, all Pamphile's family & friends had assembled at our house. I'm sure you remember when we entered the house, he came & stood before me with the most tender attitude; & you must have remarked how he gave us both a kiss on the cheek, telling me as he did that, if it wasn't for my mother, he would have come & got me out of bed himself, & chastised me for my laziness. After that, you know how all the assembly paid us their respects, in what manner the contract was drawn up, & how the ceremony went: so that it seemed there was nothing else remaining for the celebration, than the victim.

Tullie.

That is truer than you think, when you call our virginity a victim, for it is our virginity that must be immolated, or massacred, & torn to pieces with an effusion of blood.

Octavie.

All these formalities having been strictly observed,

Pamphile & I found ourselves together. That was when he asked me with quite a bit of tenderness in his voice, whether I wanted to be with him: I told him that I was no longer master of myself, that he was master of my person, & that having nothing else to give but my heart, that he should know he possessed it. Meanwhile, as I spoke, he was kissing me all over; & after a thousand caresses, he had me quite on fire: I was entirely beside myself, & I have to say that I could no longer breathe except through him. During these sweet pastimes, I had two chambermaids at my side, whom my mother had ordered to stand there, to be witnesses to what transpired between us. They lowered their eyes during all this playfulness, & didn't dare look at us straight on. "My lover," said Pamphile, addressing himself to me, "make these girls go out, their presence is not needed here; for what does any of this have to do with them?" "God forfend," I said in a low voice, "that I should be so indiscreet! Think about it: what would my mother & all my family say, if we were to be left alone?" He interrupted me by planting a thousand kisses on my mouth, face, neck, & breasts, & as soon as he did my mother came in. "Ah, Gods!", she said, "how you overwhelm my poor Octavie with your caresses! you really love her, don't you?" "Ah! do you have any doubt about it?" he said immediately, "Love itself has nothing more to add to make it more ardent: but alas! mother," he continued (speaking to Sempronie), "given you had enough goodness to give me so beautiful & pleasant a person for a wife, permit me now to exercise the rights & functions of a husband; I entreat you, grant me this favor." "You obviously have no considera-

tion," said my mother, "for Octavie's delicacy, –
she's only sixteen years old. Reflect on that a little,
my son." "Ah! have some pity on me," Pamphile took
up again; "I can't take it anymore, I'm no longer in
control of myself, & I burn inside with a fire that only
Octavie can put out: allow me then to enjoy her, & be
liberal with me with a good that belongs to me; you
cannot refuse me this, without taking from me something that is my own." She smiled at this. "You do not
consider, my son," she said to him, "how all your re-
quests are out of season: trust me, wait for that night;
this small delay will make your divertissement much
more enjoyable, than if you were to follow through
with your first sallies; with all my heart I wish," she
continued, "I could grant you what you want, but you
can see for yourself that neither the time, nor the
place, can allow it." "Ah! my very dear mother," responded Pamphile, "have compassion on your son-in-
law. Octavie is not as cruel as you; & doubtless she
will not refuse to relieve my distress, given she's the
cause of it." "Eh, well, my daughter," my mother said
to me, "do you want to cure Pamphile of his malady;
are you okay with this; what do you say?"

Tullie.

And why would you not have wanted to? You were
too wise not to consent.

Octavie.

My face blushed with modesty at first, & it prevented
me from speaking even. "What, you say nothing?"
my mother prodded, "Which means you consent.
Well! get up & walk around for a bit while I speak

with Pamphile; I have something in particular I need to speak with him about regarding you." I got up & moved away three or four paces, & I lent such an ear to their discourses that I didn't miss a single word. "My son," she said in a small voice, "you know I'm right when I say that it's neither the right time nor place for your divertissement; judge for yourself: in the other room, all our relatives & yours have arrived; there is no bed in this room; what do you pretend to do at this moment in time? I see your urgency, however," she continued; "& in order to give you some sort of satisfaction, I'm willing to put Octavie in your hands, but on the condition that she satisfies only one of your lustful desires for the moment: tomorrow night you can cull all you wish, & you'll have the leisure to enjoy at long draws the sweet nectars of marriage. I grant you, then, even though I know that Octavie has nothing in this room she can use to accommodate her, to put herself in an advantageous position, for herself or you; you will clearly be wasting your time & your oil; but it's useless preaching to you: if nothing else, be mindful of her youth. I warn you, because I've heard you have a monstrous virile member whose length & thickness could cause her much damage, if you approach this business with too much haste." There you have it, Tullie, what I heard; after which my mother called me over & said to me: "My daughter, you are no longer mistress of your own body; your husband controls you now: those are the laws of marriage. He has asked me if I might give you back to him again in order that he might satisfy, if only for one moment, his overriding disposition; neither you nor I can refuse him this request; I have agreed then; but on one condition: that he might satisfy himself on you, for the time being, once only; that's why, as soon as he has satisfied himself, you must pry yourself loose & promptly leave the room; if you do the opposite, I will be upset with you." I promised her everything she asked for. "Above all," she continued, "put yourself into whatever postures he asks you to take, but be attentive lest, by your own fault, his semen escapes & goes anywhere else than where it is supposed to be; act in such a way that when he is on top of you, not a single drop of semen falls outside." After this warning, she gave me a kiss on the cheek, & left me alone with Pamphile. We didn't lose any time, & we were already disposed for combat, when my mother came back in again, saying that she had forgotten to tell us the most important thing. Pamphile had already had me seated on a rather wide bench that was attached to the wall, & covered by a rug; he had me spread my legs & place each foot on a stool to raise them: I was naked to the navel, & my adversary already had his weapon in hand. As soon as my mother entered, & she saw me in this position: "O my God!" she said, "how love is ingenious, & how that position is suitable for the both of you!" but she was much more surprised at the sight of Pamphile's war hammer, swelled to the nth degree, ready to wage battle. "Ah! bounty of Venus!" she ejaculated, "what a monster! Brace yourself, daughter." Meanwhile, I had taken a more decent posture, & I had put down my skirts. I asked my mother what she had forgotten to tell us. "Octavie," she said to me, "as it is not necessary that those who will dine with us this evening should see your clothes soiled by your frolics, I find it appropriate to ask you to get out of your clothes entirely. On saying which, she began to undress me herself, leaving only my chemise; she kissed me; & then calling Pamphile who had stepped back a bit: "Come, my son, come," she said to him; "Take a good look at the battlefield where you must wage combat." And then she left the room laughing. As soon as Pamphile saw himself at liberty, he locked the door to the room from the inside; & throwing himself at me, he administered a thousand kisses & pulled off my chemise. As I was standing there completely naked, he walked around me & took me in with his eyes from all sides; satisfied by his sight, his hands began to touch me. He then had me sit down as before, placing each foot on a stool; then he slid his right hand under my buttocks & bringing them closer to him, he positioned his prick at the entrance to the gate of love, & he tried to penetrate me.

Tullie.

Oh boy, stiff upper lip; this is not going badly though: & what did you do?

Octavie.

Me, I remained nearly motionless; I let him do what he needed to do, & I didn't refuse him a thing: he had gotten himself naked like me. Having approached me & readied his battery vis-a-vis the place of attack, he said to me: "Octavie, my love, kiss me, then lift your right leg & press it against the small of my back." "I don't understand," I said, "what you want; I don't get it: as for the rest of it, take pity on me, I beg you." He didn't respond, & he lifted my right leg himself, according to his wishes; & at the same time he pushed in with his prick, but so rudely, so roughly, that I thought it was a death blow he had dealt me, what with all the pain it caused me: I cried out as soon as he did it. "Shh! be quiet, my love," he said to me, "You have nothing more to fear or suffer; stay like you are, & don't move." He put his hand under by buttocks again, & inserted his prick into my vagina, but with so much violence that I cried out again, even louder than before. My mother, who was in the adjoining room, ran to the door. She tried the handle, then rapped softly. "Eh, what's going on in there, Pamphile?" she said. "Is that what you promised me just now? I gave you a romp, not a full scale battle." She said no more: Pamphile discharged, right as she was saying this, & I felt a wetness at the entrance to my cunt, as if it were a warm rain falling. Then he pushed with even more vehemence, & that viscous humor favored his attack: he advanced two or three inches in length, & his semen spilled all over the place he had entered; to the degree that it became too abundant, & it was flowing outside of me; my pubic hair got all wet.

Tullie.

And then!? You stayed motionless all this time? You did not feel a thing? & you did not come as valiantly as he did?

Octavie.

I confess, my dear Tullie, that I was just beginning to understand what is meant by the pleasures of Venus. When Pamphile stirred like this between my legs, I felt inside me such a large itch that, no longer mistress of myself, I pushed & pulled my buns with such an incredible fury; something came out, at that instant, I don't know what, which caused me such an intense feeling of pleasure that I cannot explain it to you. The stimulation was so sweet, the superabundance of pleasure so great, that I was dying; & with languishing looks, I let out several sighs: my face was flushed, my cunt was on fire, & my entire body was extremely heavy & exhausted. "Ah! ah! ah! my dear Pamphile," I said, "I'm dying, I cannot do this anymore; hold on to my soul: it's about to leave my body: ah, Gods! my how death is voluptuous!" "Buck up, buck up," he said to me in response, "my dear child; we're going to start a new combat now: gather your strength, & me I'm going to pick up my weapon again." He did what he said in effect; picking up his war hammer which he had pulled out of me, he then put it back into the hole. "Funny thing, Tullie!" he said, "I had only just put it back in, when it excited a new passion in me, & I made such a copious discharge that it seemed more like urine than semen that was rushing out of me; it came out with such impetuosity!" Ah! if Pamphile had been in form at that moment, I truly believe we would have enjoyed the perfect pleasure. I was quite displeased with him that he had finished his romp so quickly.

Tullie.

You say things so naively that I am beside myself by your discourse; you have set me all afire. Kiss me, my love, embrace me, my dear Cléante! I cannot stand it anymore, I am burning up, I do not know what I want; ah! kiss me!

Octavie.

What do you mean by "my dear Cléante?" There's some mystery for sure. What do you want? What do you desire from me?

Tullie.

Ah, please, my little cutie, my dear child, help me out a little here, your poor Tullie: give me your hand.

Octavie.

Here you go; what do you want it for?

Tullie.

Put it there, ah, I beg you, in that place that is all on fire; push your finger in as far as you can; be my husband, my dear Octavie, & I will be your wife; climb up on me; & by your bumps & by your shocks, try to extinguish the fire that you have excited in me by your discourse. Good, that is good, there you go, excellent; shake now, while I am holding you. Ah! how our two pussies are joined one to the other! ah! how I like it when you do that! again, stronger, harder; ah! I cannot take it any more, I am coming, I am coming: ah! Push, Cléante, push, I'm coming, ah! ah! ah!

Octavie.

Ah, Gods! how lubricious you are! I believe that love itself would drown in this torrent of semen that exits from your cunt. Ah! I feel I don't know how to describe it; ah, ah, my very dear, my love, let's die together then, the two of us. Who could have imagined that this playfulness would have been followed by such sweet pleasure? Ah! I'm coming again! ah, ah, ah, I swoon...

Tullie.

I am delighted you have shared this pleasure with me. Look at me, thanks to Venus, a bit relaxed now: let us get back to Pamphile, whom you left in a fury in the assault on your fortress.

Octavie.

I'd like nothing better; but before I do, tell me what you mean by Cléante, & to what purpose you were imploring his aid. For why not call rather on your dear Oronte, who is so pleasant, & who loves you so tenderly?

Tullie.

I will tell you in good time: I will let you in on one of my most secret thoughts, & you will enter into the knowledge of one of my most hidden pleasures; & if you wish even, you may share in them with me. But I do not want to interrupt you now; continue your discourse, & remind me some other time about what I promised you.

Octavie.

I won't forget, because I'm quite curious to hear it: but back to our story. Even though Pamphile's virile member had become paralytic, & it seemed to ask for a truce, with head lowered, it didn't stop menacing me still with its thickness & its prodigious length. It was entirely covered with that dew that he & I had abundantly shed; & from one moment to the next, it grew animated again & approached the gate, as if to breach a new entrance. But, because I recognized that he was tired, & that that was enough for one round, I said to him: "Well, Pamphile, are you content now? You don't want to wear out a girl like me with your furious attacks, do you? Rest for a while, & think about the request my mother made of you." "Don't worry," he said to me, "I don't give up so easily;" & while he spoke, he kissed me & fondled me everywhere with extraordinary passion. This playing around excited him, he began to get hard again, & he prepared for new assaults when adroitly I slipped out of his arms. He pursued me immediately; as I was running around in the room to get away from him, I knocked over a bench with my foot; my mother heard it & came rapping on the door again. Pamphile quickly handed me my chemise which was completely soaked in semen; he put on his own & opened the door. "Well," she said to Pamphile when she entered, "how goes it? Clearly," she continued, "you're a valiant soldier; but I'm afraid that, for all that, you have wasted your time: it's clear to me you're a man of your word & that you wanted to return my daughter to me in the same condition I had given her to you." She mocked him like that, because she had realized that he had hardly made any headway; not to mention that I believe she had watched us through the keyhole.

Tullie.

Really, you should not doubt it at all: the most saintly of women have curiosity about all sorts of things; & I will tell you that the day that followed the first night of my honeymoon I was obligated to recount to my mother point by point everything that had taken place between me & my husband. She even wanted me to apprise her of the smallest acts of playfulness. While I recounted these things to her, she embraced me & kissed me with unparalleled tenderness.

Octavie.

Sempronie was none the less curious. You should know that not long after she entered the room, Pamphile retired into the next one with his clothes, so that she could be alone with me. She closed the door behind him, & throwing her arms around my neck, she said "Eh, well, my dear Octavie, you've had quite a time of it, yes? Do you have anything you're ashamed to tell me? The interest I take in everything that regards you obliges you to reveal everything that you can to me, to give me some joy." On saying this, she kissed me, she was all hot; her eyes exuded love, & I could tell by her countenance that she was feeling strange emotions.

Tullie.

That should not surprise you: because aside from the fact that Sempronie is of a strongly amorous temperament, she is barely twenty-nine years old; she was married when she was thirteen, she became pregnant in the same year, & she gave birth to you just after she turned fourteen.

Octavie.

I said nothing to her in response; but she pressured me so much that I was obliged to satisfy her. "Ah well!" I said to her, "I obeyed you, & I gave Pamphile what he wanted." "Which is? Speak freely to me, daughter," she responded: "The fact of the matter is that you are, right now, no more than a child; it's enough that you & I are women, so as not to lack in judgment, for our husbands give us wit in the same way they give us pleasure."

Tullie.

She is right, & I have seen girls who, quite uncouth & stupid, became more spiritual & quite enlightened as soon as they tasted the sweetness of marriage.

Octavie.

I'm of quite the same mind; & in fact it seems that our spirit is reclused & closed up with our virginity. When we are girls, whatever smarts we might have then, we know only the rough exterior & the superficial nature of things; a chimera can make us afraid, the slightest things frighten us, & the only person who can pick that flower is the man capable of enlightening us. *Qui aperit vulvam, aperit & mentem.* That is to say that he alone opens our mind, who opens our vagina. It seems that when we are born, nature gives us no other location for our understanding than between our legs, & which is more in accordance with its operations; it needs strong effort, violent jolts, & pushes to raise it from its lower position & put it into our head.

Tullie.

Very nice, very nice: ah, ah, ah! as much to say that without Pamphile you would be ignorant, & that it is his prick that gave you wit. *Mentula mentem incussit.*

Octavie.

Having become a little bolder by my mother's discourse then, I spoke a bit more freely: "I am," I told
her, "the same as when I entered; nothing's happened
to me, except that Pamphile has gotten me wet all
over." "What!" she said, "he hasn't advanced at all?"
"No," I said, "because in addition to his prick being
too thick to enter, it lost its energy after several
thrusts, losing its seed." "That doesn't sound good,"
my mother responded: "Show me your chemise." I
showed it to her; as soon as she saw it: "O, my daughter," she exclaimed, "do you realize what you have
missed out on? Ah! How happy you would be if so
abundant a shower had drenched you on the inside.
Yes, my cute little girl," she continued while looking
attentively at the stains on my chemise; "there would
have been enough here to give us an heir as robust as
Hercules." She made me get out of it; after that, she
gave me another one, fixed up my hair again, & did
everything she could to make me look more glam-
orous & presentable.

Tullie.

What did she do with the chemise you got out of? I
think she examined it closely

Octavie.

Of course: she examined it every which way; I was
not in the least bit ashamed. "It's a deluge, my child,"
she said to me, "that you have endured, & not a simple shower: but what happened that made you shout
so loudly? Because I see no sign of blood for your
virginity. Clearly," she continued, "the stronghold
was attacked, but he was not able to make himself

master of the place; have courage: I hope that things will go better tonight." And with that, she retired, & locked my dirty chemise in her cabinet.

Tullie.

Night has its pleasures as well as day; & the entertainments they offer us are much purer than others, given that tranquillity reigns at night. I am not going to ask you want happened at dinner; tell me instead what happened on that amorous night that aroused you both to unparalleled heights.

Octavie.

We began to come alive as soon as daylight expired; & as soon as we had seen to the importunate visits that customarily are frequent at these types of celebrations, finally we were able to catch our breath, Pamphile & I. You know, for you were present, as my mother took us both by the hand & conducted us to the room where the bed was prepared, where I was going to be so well treated. But I forgot to tell you that a little while before this, she shut herself in that room with me, where my maidenhead had suffered its first attacks. As soon as I had entered I could smell the odor of a certain perfume that was extremely sweet & agreeable. "Lift you skirts & your chemise to the navel," my mother said to me. I obeyed her immediately; as soon as she saw me naked, she smiled; "One has to admit, Octavie," she said to me, "that you are made for Pamphile. You must," she continued, "in order to spare the both of you lots of pain & trouble, rub this liquor on your vagina. At that same moment, she pulled out a small vermillion bottle with gold trim on it; I dipped two fingers into it; & after having retracted them totally covered with that perfume, I touched my "invention," greasing it all around. "Not your pubic hair; not your *mons Veneris;* inside, silly: you need to rub it inside." Whereupon she dipped her own finger into the jar & applied this marvelous unction to my nether part herself; she penetrated me with her finger as far as she could go. "I was," she said, "stronger than you are when I got married to your father, & for all that, I would never have been able to endure your father if this same ointment had not been applied to my vagina." I confess, cousin, that this unction had a prodigious effect on me & surprised me; it caused such a great stimulation in my vagina, & so sweet a feeling, that I felt nearly beside myself: for it didn't take long before I had forgotten who I was entirely, & I ran to Pamphile to engage him in battle.

Tullie.

These strong ointments are almost always resorted to, particularly when the girl who is married is young & delicate.

Octavie.

What more do you want? You know all this as you took me to bed; & in order to help me with these matters, as it was you who said the last goodbye to my virginity. As soon as Pamphile saw that he was alone with me, he closed the door to the chamber, with the design of opening mine, & he looked everywhere, & conducted an exact research, to determine if there wasn't anyone hidden anyplace.

Tullie.

That is a strange thing to do, as this sort of game has no lack of witnesses; *& tamen sine testibus non agitur*: which is to say that it cannot be achieved, if the Divinities who are the witnesses of virility are not in on it.

Octavie.

After you had exited the room, my mother asked me if had any fear; I told her that I did not fear anything from anyone I loved: she added, that if I wanted, she would speak with my husband to go easy on me a little; I responded that I would gladly suffer all those bad treatments, if he could draw pleasure from it. Pamphile, who was standing at a distance from us, lent an ear, & he heard all this conversation. My mother exited & bid us a happy night, & he immediately came to me precipitously, & embracing me tightly, he said to me: "Ah! I am so obliged to you, my dearest, that you want to put yourself in my hands under no conditions! You will lose nothing thereby; I promise you already, in return for your love, that I will do nothing without your consent. I hope also," he continued, that you will be complaisant enough not to refuse me anything." "Alas," I responded, "what resistance could I employ against the person I cherish the most in the world! His servants had already undressed him; he had only his chemise on, with a jacket; he got rid of them both quickly, & jumped into bed completely nude. It was then that he embraced me with an unparalleled ardor & kissed me a thousand times: he fondled my breasts, he touched my belly & thighs, & he did all that with such brusque movements & transport of joy that it was easy to see he was no longer in control of himself.

Tullie.

What the...! Did he forget the most important part? That which was supposed to make him most happy, – Was it left out of his caresses?

Octavie.

No, but that's where he ended up; *mille viae ducunt homines per saecula Romam*, as they say; he fondled it like all the other parts of my body, he put his fingers inside, he kissed it even; & on smelling the odor that it was perfumed with, he smiled: "Ah, my love!" he said to me, "you are all roses & myrrh; I know quite well that it's Sempronie who wanted to make this route of sensual delight easier to attack. I also want," he continued (while exposing his long, thick, & reddish penis to me), "art to assist nature in me; & in order for this redoubtable instrument to do its duty with less pain, I will rub a jasmine pomade on it, which I brought with me for this very purpose: & you, o my Goddess! prepare to defend yourself, & to sustain as needed the attacks I wish to wage against you."

Tullie.

Ah! I beg all the Gods & Goddesses that preside over hymen, in a word, all the divinities that have been receptive to Love, to assist you at this rude moment.

Octavie.

I think that if I was waiting for assistance from that quarter, I would have soon lost patience.

Tullie.

You do not know apparently that marriage was not consecrated in the past, except when there were three or four divinities present, who had each his or her own particular office on that day. The Goddess of Virginity, who was to begin the ceremony, & who undid the belt of the newlywed; she was followed by another who placed the husband & wife on the field of battle; they called him God Subigus: another presided over the action, particularly when the husband, mounted on his woman, pushed her vigorously; that was the Goddess Praema: finally, the last of these official divinities is named the Goddess Pertunda: her specialty is making the man's prick enter the woman's vagina more easily.

Octavie.

Really, they needed so many ceremonies in the past then to take a girl's maidenhead? One doesn't need so many nowadays; & Pamphile, without any Gods' assistance, got on just fine; it was no more difficult for him than any other, I think: listen, here's how he took it: You know, Tullie, that he's quite young, for he is barely twenty-two years old; but he is strong; having put me then in the ordinary posture, he spread my legs & removed my hand, which was covering the place he wanted to enter: it is true that I didn't make much of a fuss. That done, he threw himself at me: that new charge frightened me a little; he noticed it. "Don't be afraid," he said, "my dear child, only be strong: these words were followed up by a furious thrust, which inserted the head of his penis completely inside my vagina. This act was so violent that I thought he had torn me to shreds; I put my hand there to prevent him from going any further, but Pamphile opposed it: "Remove," he said to me, "your hand, which gets in the way of our pleasure; be courageous, the road to arrive at the height of felicity is nearly traveled."

Tullie.

What did you do?

Octavie.

I held firmly, between my hands, the rest of his penis, which hadn't yet entered, & I held on to it strongly while he renewed his attack. "Ah! my love," he said to me, "squeeze, empalm, hold it as tightly as possible. I feel that I'm incontinent after having wet all your insides with a celestial rain. Pamphile stopped moving; & what surprised me the most was that he didn't lose a single drop of that liquor, which had only just been scattered about when I felt the canal it had just exited from grow flaccid, & it shrank in my hands almost by half the size of what it was a moment earlier.

Tullie.

Was there a light in your room at that time?

Octavie.

Of course, & one could see as clearly as if it were midday: "That was nice, sweetiepie," Pamphile said to me, "Ah! I really enjoyed that! But do you want," he continued, "to rest a little?" "Yes," I said to him: & immediately he stopped fucking me; but the strangest thing then happened! He had only just pulled out his dick when I felt an incredible itch inside: it was so great that, unable to contain myself any longer, I threw my arms around his neck, I kissed him, I embraced him, & I tried to get him hard again by my sighs. He wasn't at all insensitive to all that; & answering caress for caress, he played with my vagina which was all hot & on fire; he opened my lips, then closed them again, & did suchlike & so forth until I came all of a sudden, but with such force that all my seed flowed outside, together with everything that was inside me. That surprised Pamphile: "Who would have thought," he said to me, "my dear Octavie, tender & young as you are, that you would be so sensual, & so amenable to pleasure? Most girls your age," he continued, "are not the least bit affected by the first attacks; but here you are ravished all the way to Heaven & back! No," he said, while looking carefully at the semen I had just discharged, "this is not a simple outflow, it's a deluge! & clearly you must have inside you lively sources of this liquid, to be able to produce such abundant ejaculations. Ah, how naturally playful you are!" he said to me: "all this semen you see spilled here, – it's not mine; it's what you responded with. No matter," he continued, "whether yours or mine: I'm just delighted you could share in the pleasure, & that you have experienced it to the full. I have no cause to complain," he added, "& I'm sufficiently indemnified for the difficulties & grief you caused me at the start with your first fits of rage." My mother had forgotten to place any linen under the pillow, so I used the sheets to dry myself, & to clean myself up with. The semen was everywhere. "The next time, my dear Octavie," said Pamphile to me, after he had seen how things turned out, "I want you to do all that I ask you to, for my pleasure, & I hope that everything I find enjoyable you will too." "I understand," I told him, "& I consent in advance to whatever you want me to do; but, for goodness' sake, spare me a little shame & don't make me do those shameless movements & acts that fatigue the body & the mind." "No, no," he took up again, "that's not at all what I want; just the opposite: I don't want you to move at all in fact: just lie there, on your back, & don't move."

Tullie.

A husband is allowed to lay down the law as he pleases with his wife, & it is prudent for her to observe the rules without saying so much as a word; she is a sot if she imagines that there is anything unseemly in the obedience she renders him.

Octavie.

I obeyed him without much ceremony; he entreated me to hold on to his cock which was starting to grow hard again; I did it as soon as he asked me to; what can I say? I worked it up into a such a feverish state that he climbed onto me & performed so well that, on the first attempt, he entered me halfway. Five inches of his little man still remained outside though; that pissed him off, for it seemed he had wanted to stuff it all inside me. "And it is at this moment," he said to me, "my dear, that I must ask you to do something: count all my thrusts, & be very attentive you don't miss a single one of them." As soon as he said this, he pushed higher; & while I was amusing myself counting, he redoubled his efforts with such violence that he broke through the barricade; he made himself master of the place, & he entered the citadel in all his glory. But the pain that I felt just then prevented me from counting. "Ah! you're killing me," I told him, "you're killing me; pull out, I beg you, that instrument of pain that has wounded me so." "Eh, please!... Not on your life. Far from it." he retorted, "Indeed: I plan to advance as far as I can," & on saying this, he thrust at me so rudely that he pushed himself entirely up inside me; his pubic hair was touching mine, & we had never been so better united, as at that moment. "Ah! stop," I shouted, "I cannot take it anymore, you're piercing me through & through; you are touching the bottom of my entrails; ah! I can no longer put up a fight!" He felt a little compassion for me, & pulled his cock out by half: "What is it, my poor little wife," he asked me, "have I touched the back of the canal? Keep up the good fight, don't be afraid, & the game will be over before you know it." While saying this, he pushed imperceptibly, & advanced his man again. "When you feel," he continued, "some pain, tell me immediately, my dear child, & I'll pull back; I love you too much to want to extract my pleasure at the expense of your pain, & in this way to turn my lust into cruelty." And after saying that he pushed in his rod with such a violence, that I had to say something: "Stop," I said, "I beg you: what good does it do to push with such force? I cannot take it anymore." Another four inches & he would have been lodged completely inside me again. "I understand now," he said to me, "just how much prick is needed in order not to hurt you, & I think that, provided it remains three inches on the outside, you will not be indisposed; but you need to do something: I want you to grip my penis with your hand, whatever remains outside; squeeze it as hard as you can; you must make up with your hand for your body's insufficiency: don't be ashamed at all," he proceeded; "because every inch of the flesh on a beautiful girl like you is nothing but a delicious fuck." I obeyed him, & he moved so well, that on the tenth push, he discharged; I felt a small tingling feeling inside, but that was all.

Tullie.

How many blows did you count this time, on your second round?

Octavie.

Twenty, before he upset the count, & ten after that: but I don't really know the exact number; for after I cried out that he was killing me, that he was hurting me, he pushed in with even greater force: why? I have no idea.

Tullie.

And how did you spend the rest of the night?

Octavie.

The rest of the night was spent playing around. Pamphile was stretched out on top of me; he took pleasure in making me suck his cock, to the very last drop; he kissed me & hugged me, when all of a sudden we heard someone opening the door next to the bed: it was my mother, who started to laugh as soon as she saw us. "Eh, well," she said, "are you enjoying yourselves now?" "Ah, mother," I said to her, "you have put me in the hands of an uncomfortable man. He hasn't let me alone all night, & I haven't had a moment's rest." "You're quite upset about it, I can see that," she responded, laughing: then addressing herself to Pamphile, she said: "Eh well, brave soldier, is it a woman you are in bed with now?" "Octavie," he said, "has some news to tell you; don't you see her all afflicted for having lost her virginity?" "It's only now, then," said my mother, "that I recognize in you a son, & as my son-in-law." She handed each of us a bowl of restorative bouillon, to help us regain the strength we had lost: she blew out the candles that were lit at the base of the bed, & then she retired. As soon as she had left, Pamphile embraced me tightly; & after several caresses, because we were both tired & fatigued, sleep got the better of us both, & we slept for a rather long time. Day had already broken when, on waking, I noticed Pamphile's body completely uncovered; I have to tell you in good faith, my dear Tullie, that I looked at him & considered him from head to foot, with an extraordinary curiosity. No, I don't believe that one could find a more handsome & more lovable man: all parts of his body had an unparalleled regularity of shape. He was asleep on his back so that I could observe him at my leisure; his arms are long & of a perfect roundness; his belly slightly raised; his legs not too fat, nor too thin: in sum, he's a natural work of art. His skin is white, & without imperfection: one would have thought, on seeing him like this, that he was a marble statue. *Il Gigante* himself.

Tullie.

Pamphile's cock was asleep too? You have not said

anything about it.

Octavie.

Can you believe it, Tullie? His penis is redoubtable even during repose; it appeared to menace me; but what surprised me the most was that the more I looked at it, the harder it got; I watched it so attentively; it grew animated, & spirited. It seemed fully capable of conceiving some feelings of glory, for having been thus looked at by its mistress; it moved & lifted its head several times. It had a mind of its own. These agitations finally woke Pamphile; & me, as soon as I realized it, I pretended to be deeply asleep: he turned over on his side. "Do you," he said to me, "still sleep, my cutie?" "Ah, why?" I responded, "are you interrupting my rest?" Meanwhile he kissed me, embraced me, fondled me; & after having regarded me up & down, with the most loving & lascivious eyes in the world, he climbed up on top of me again & began to fuck me, while reminding me of my promise, that is, not to move. I enjoyed this last round quite a bit, & the stimulation I felt was so great, that I broke my word, & I could not prevent from shaking my ass with unbelievable speed. As soon as he noticed, he redoubled his attack, & pushed his prick into me up to the hilt; but I didn't feel any pain this time; I let out only a small sigh; immediately afterwards I was soaked with a liquid balm, which succeeded in healing me of all my ills. Pamphile swore that he had never enjoyed so perfect a voluptuousness before, than at this moment. And that, my very dear cousin, is how we passed the night; & after several more words were exchanged, we went back to sleep until about eleven o'clock in the morning, when we were woken; you know the rest as well as I do.

Tullie.

Pamphile is not so brave a knight as I thought: to make three rounds in the night, with so beautiful a mount as you are, ah! that's being cowardly. How can he be content with so few! That said, Octavie, I'm not surprised, when I reflect on the size of his penis; for it is a well-known fact that almost all men whose prick exceeds the natural size are not as good a lay as others.

Octavie.

I don't doubt it, cousin; but I'm surprised that men are not always ready for combat, given there's nothing so sweet as the pleasure one enjoys by it: they are slackers if we compare them to ourselves; we enjoy sex much more than they do; we are much more sensitive to it, & much more prompt to come.

Tullie.

I hear you; you draw these truths from the warmth you sustained during Pamphile's heated assaults on your maidenhead: you would not be Sempronie's daughter, in fact, if you were not as amorous as she is; & you would have nothing in common with her, if you had not the same penchant for sex.

Octavie.

It's a sign of her virtue that she overcame this weakness so well: because whatever inclination she had or has for such entertainments, she's done nothing that could make anyone accuse her of being a lubricious woman.

Tullie.

It is very clear to me, Octavie, that you do not know her like I do. Do you want me to tell you what I know?

Octavie.

I'd like nothing better.

Tullie.

You should know then that Sempronie, from a very early age, was taken with pleasure; that Lucretie, Victorie, & I, who conversed each day with her, became the most lascivious girls in the city because of her. We were nine or ten years old then, & Sempronie was twelve; she liked Victorie a lot, & had quite tender feelings for Lucretie & me as well. She joined us in all our puerile entertainments, & treated us as if we were boys, rather than girls: she called us her lovers; she said she wanted to teach us how to make love; she gazed at us with languishing eyes, batting her eyes; she claimed that we were dearer to her than anyone or thing in the world; that she was out of her mind in love with us, that she was on fire, & that we were the only ones would could extinguish her flames. All these amorous declarations were followed by a thousand kisses & caresses. Too young to be sensitive to all this playfulness, we could do nothing but laugh at all her carryings-on, & innocently granted to Sempronie all that she desired from us. We spent nearly every afternoon together, playing these kinds of games, & sometimes she slipped her hand under our skirts & fondled, with an incredible passion, that part of our body that distinguishes us from men. She inserted her fingers, one after the other, into our ***[5] & kissed us at the same time, sliding her tongue between our lips with extreme desire: sometimes these games went even farther; because she made us bend over & touch the ground, then she trussed up our skirts above the hips, & got a good look at our nudity, both in front & from behind. She touched our butts, pinched them, bit them, kissed them even with surprising transports of feeling; finally, there was nothing she didn't touch when she was in one of her passionate fits. I remember she sometimes played the school teacher & the governess; & after making us lift our skirts, she whipped us with canes & rods if we broke any of the rules of the game: she often made our buttocks sting; when she did, we got upset with her; & to appease us, she got completely undressed in front of us, & obliged us to do the same to her. To avenge ourselves of the harm she had done us, we whipped her one after the other; she suffered it with great patience, even though she made some faces for form's sake. I have to tell you, Octavie, she had a beautiful body; there was nothing whiter, firmer, smoother; her buns were admirably round & tight. But let me get back to our story: after we had all grown quite tired of whipping her, she got up, & told us it was her turn. She made us lie down on our back, on wooden cases; she made us open our legs; & after some fondling, she jumped our bones (remember that we were completely nude) & pressing her part up against ours, she shook & moved as if she were a boy. Well, Octavie,

---

[5]Editor's note: ***: this word has been removed to preserve some semblance of propriety. Those who wish to read it will need to resort to the French (or Latin).

anyone who has a mother like that – how can she not be like Venus? eh, eh, eh... What do you think?

Octavie.

I think I would have to agree, Tullie, with what you just said, provided you can make me understand how, with so great a penchant for sex, my mother, from such a tender age until now, has never done anything that has diminished her honor.

Tullie.

Ah, ah, I will gladly explain that to you; listen to me then. Three or four months before Sempronie got married, we were one afternoon all together enjoying ourselves; her father & her mother were absent from the house; they had left her alone with her governess, who was at that moment occupied with the affairs of the house, so much so that Sempronie was free to do as she liked, & had nothing to fear from anyone. She had a small page of fourteen years old, by the name of Joconde; he was pretty like an angel, & his mind was as sharp as his body was beautiful; he was talented; he sang agreeably, & he danced with marvelous skill. Sempronie, who presided over our games, said that he had to join the group; we consented to this with joy, because he was really quite a nice boy: she then made him approach, after making sure the coast was clear. As soon as he had entered our circle, he sang & danced with particular charm; but the game didn't stop there. Sempronie had quite another idea in mind; it is why she interrupted him with each step he made: she pushed him while he was in the middle of a dance; & she excited him, by a thousand attacks &

prods & pushes, to a very different sort of entertainment. "O the beautiful girl," she said to us, showing him off; "My how pretty she is! Isn't she pretty? How lovely she is! Look, my good companions, look what a good girl she is, & so very modest. I swear to you," she continued, "that this is not a boy, but a young virgin, who dishonors our sex by wearing boy's clothing." Joconde defended himself at first by some rather spirited retorts; but Sempronie said such things to him, after repeated assaults, that she succeeded in pushing him to the edge: his face reddened, as boys sometimes do, & tried to get away from us, by fleeing: but it was useless, he was no match for the four of us; & by running after him, we had soon recovered the fugitive. We brought him to the foot of the bed (for we were playing inside the house), which was inside the room. "Ah! now, now is the time," said Sempronie, "for us to see whether she is a girl or a boy." No sooner said than done: she slipped her hand into the opening of his knee breeches.

Octavie.

What!? & what did Joconde do? Did he defend himself at all? ah! ah! ah!

Tullie.

"Take back your hand," he said to her, defending himself lightly; if you're not careful, I too will see if you are a virgin or not." Meanwhile Sempronie did not let go of her prize, she continued to hold in her hands the instrument of that little Adonis; & having pulled it out, she made us touch it, Victorie & me. Poor innocent girls that we were, we looked at it attentively; we wondered how it worked, when, by Sempronie's fondling, it grew larger & longer under our very eyes. "Well, Joconde," your mother said to him, "what have you got to say for yourself now?"...[6]

Octavie.

So what did he have to say for himself?

Tullie.

I will tell you another time. But tell me, you do know, don't you, that we Italian women are, as a general rule, extremely fuckable from our most tender youth?

Octavie.

If you say so, but you'll need to make an exception for you & me; because I could not be deflowered without sensible suffering, & you told me yourself that you also experienced some pain.

Tullie.

You are right, of course. We have married two men who are extremely well-endowed; which is why it is not surprising that we appeared tight to men who could not find women too large for them. Oronte & Pamphile can dispute who is larger between themselves; I think they could even give Priapus a run for his money; & if the good matrons of Lampsakos had gotten a hold of them after that Phallic hero was deified, they would not have deplored his absence as much as they did. You know about Priapus, yes? Here

---

[6]Editor's note: The rest of this passage of several pages has been cut to preserve some semblance of propriety. Besides, we believe the law would not allow it. Those who wish to read it will need to resort to the French (or Latin).

is what they say about him:

> *The pleasure I take cannot be small,*
> *Never do I f*** crustaceans;*
> *And the reason is that my Prick*
> *Can never find a Cunt large enough.*

If we can believe the stories they tell, he was a Lord Master; well! I believe our husbands can boast as much, because they carry the day over all the other pricks in the world. Sempronie & Victorie have confessed to me also that on the first night of their nuptials they got off easy, without any pain, whatever side they were on; what is certain however is that neither of their husbands are badly endowed: it is the result of something else. You must have no doubt about it, Octavie; & it is also true that Italian & Spanish women are so large that it seems they were born more for mules than for men. Joconde had already opened their passage, & that may be what made entry so easy for them.

Octavie.

I guess so: I hadn't thought about it.

Tullie.

Alas! I'm joking. The poor boy had nothing longer than one's middle finger at the time; & the thickness of his prick was like that of my thumb. And as for men, physicians say those who have more than seven or eight inches in length exceed the limits of nature: & the reason they give is, they say, that the neck of the womb ordinarily cannot stretch to such lengths during the course of the Venereal act; that a longer extension than that cannot be made without great travail, or without inconveniencing the woman. It is the same with thickness: because after the male's virile member has inflated & become furious, as sometimes happens, the whole business cannot be concluded without incredible pain & suffering on the part of the woman mounted. And that, Octavie, is what I have to tell you about your mother Sempronie, & our entertainments as children. Did you like it? Is your curiosity satisfied?

Octavie.

You betcha, & you have taught me things that surprise me to the nth degree. Until now, I had thought that there was no woman more saintly than my mother, & whose mores were more irreproachable; but I see now it's quite the opposite; & I have no idea how she pulled it off, given that my father, who is a very suspicious man, & who has an extraordinarily refined sensibility in points of honor, never saw anything in her that was not laudable. He's head over heels in love with her, you know, & he thinks she's the best & most honest woman in the world: but what's more surprising, the gossip-mongering that spares no one, & which spreads around our most secret vices, has never censured her behavior, nor discovered in her the least default that might have sparked criticism.

Tullie.

That should not surprise you: a prudent person always knows how to arrange things; & the greater part of women who fall by the wayside should not at all attribute the cause to their entertainments, but only to a small lack of precaution. There are those who are not content with being admired quietly; they draw glory from their infamy & prefer to hear a bit of mud slung at themselves, than to not hear anything spoken about them at all. That there is the true road to perdition; for you must know, Octavie, that praise or blame does not consist in the inherent nature of some act or thing: no, it is only what people say about it or us that matters; & with prudence we can set limits on ourselves, in order not to be blinded by our appetites, & so as to avoid giving others the opportunity to speak about us as if we acted without rule & judgment. Think about this, my dear Octavie: that if you want to live happily & content in the state of marriage, as you currently do, you must believe that there is nothing that is not permitted, & that all things are forbidden. That must seem a bit obscure to you.

Octavie.

Yes, it does; because I cannot conceive of something I might do as both permitted & forbidden at one & the same time.

Tullie.

Know then for now that everything you can do easily, without offending the eyes of your domestics & your husband, is permitted; & contrariwise, whatever you cannot do without peril, is forbidden. There, in two words, how you must regulate all your actions; those there are the veritable maxims that you must follow if you want to be wise, & it is to them alone that I owe all my pleasure & all my entertainments. It is only through practice of them, Octavie, that I have conserved my honor & my reputation; you can do the same; if you observe these rules. We are all equally driven to sensual desire, we have all the same penchants; both good & bad: but it is worth remarking that these should pose no trouble whatsoever to our reputation; they prefer pleasure to all things, & this is what makes them look villainous. There are wise women to be found among the others; but there are also imprudent women who, taking false steps, perish for the most part in the flower of their youth, or finish their days in the darkness & obscurity of a prison, where poison & iron are the instruments of punishment for their too open conduct. It is quite different for those whose characters are guided by prudence: they live happy lives until their last breath; & the circumspection they employ in all their actions makes them pass for saints in the most infamous of places, in the middle of a bordello even. You see, Octavie, that there are several paths that lead to the same end, which is pleasure, & that it is a woman's wisdom that leads her to follow the less trodden one. You understand all this quite well.

Octavie.

Yes, Tullie, & I will be obliged to you my entire life, for these good & spiritual instructions: please continue.

Tullie.

As soon as I was married, I applied myself in particular to get to know my husband's temperament; I examined his penchants & his inclinations, & I forgot nothing I had learned in order to come to a perfect understanding. After that, I considered three things: what was above me, what was outside me, & what was beneath me. I regarded religion as elevated above all things; & as it holds first place in politics (even though in nature it holds no place whatsoever), I made a serious reflection on all the duties it bound me to. I then took stock of what I owed others, & finally what I owed myself. I knew then that it was necessary that married women be strongly religious, or at minimum that they have the appearance of it; for you must know that she who is not virtuous within, provided she makes a pretense to seem so on the outside, is preferable to someone who is in fact, but who does not appear so. The happiness of a woman depends entirely on her husband's esteem; she is happy if she can pass in his mind for good & honest: but she is miserable if her too open behavior gives rise to suspicions of misbehavior. At the start of our marriage, we married couples love each other & cherish each other because of our beauty, & for other exterior charms that are found in our person: but when the first rages of love & passion have passed, there is nothing left for us but a love of esteem; that is, if our comportment appears to be without reproach & if they believe us to be proof against gallantry.

Octavie.

I am beginning, cousin, to understand this moral; this great pretense of mores shocks me.

Tullie.

Ah, then it will be all the harder to make you submit

to it! You should know there is only glory to be had by pretending to be virtuous; one cannot veil oneself with anything more precious, & all the wisdom of the female sex cannot find a surer way of enjoying a life of sexual pleasure.

Octavie.

What! A woman must abandon herself then to all sorts of vices, & have no regard for virtue?

Tullie.

Ah, Gods! you are not following me at all; far from having no regard for virtue, she must make every open profession of it, but in such a way that she is careful not to glorify bad conduct. She must temper that austerity of apparent mores, by so much gentleness & charm that without seeming to wish to please anyone, she is agreeable to everyone. Far from scorning laws & customs that are established by long usage, she must hold them in veneration, & observe them with such exact regularity that her exterior life differs in no material way from honesty, while under this veil she seeks out her entertainment. She must appear to be a mirror of saintliness on the outside, while those whom she desires to make happy will confess that there is no one more lascivious. This conduct will surprise you perhaps: but you will find that it is less harmful to civil society than the practices of saintly & devout women, who have no better purpose than to make her seem evil; & which they do, they say, in the name of virtue. O beautiful virtue, which transforms good into evil! There you have it, Octavie, the endgame of the morality that I propose to you: *Palàm vive omnibus, olàm & in tuto tibi*: that is to say, you must follow the advice of wise men, & the customs of the people, all the while keeping your most secret thoughts & actions to yourself; you must sacrifice the outside to it & all exterior appearances. It will be easy for you to observe all this; you have only to imitate your mother Sempronie.

Octavie.

I understand everything you're telling me, Tullie; but why propose my mother to me as an example?

Tullie.

You must know, Octavie, that your mother is as known to me as you are; I have suffered her playfulness, as you have mine; & here are the rules that she prescribed to me as soon as I was married. "You must regard Oronte," she told me, "like a divinity on earth; you must cherish him & adore him almost, & make yourself complaisant to all his demands, without thinking to yourself that there is anything dishonest in them. There you have it, Tullie," she said to me, "the prerogatives & the privileges of men; & there you have the advantages of women. A woman must believe, if she is clever, that because she was born to please her husband, then all other men in the world exist to please her. The first one is her own & belongs to her by right; the others are held in common just like her spouse is by other women. She must change her outward appearance as much as Proteus, in order to please him, if lubricity demands it of her: in a word, she must neglect nothing that might satisfy his lust; while her lovers employ all their skill to satisfy hers. There you have it, Octavie, in a nutshell, just how I manage Oronte, & how I behave at the same time with Cléante.

Octavie.

Excellent, excellent; Now I understand what your business with Cléante is all about.

Tullie.

It is necessary, Octavie, that I paint for you, in as few words as possible, a perfect picture of my behavior; listen to me. From the moment I got married, I have been sharing my time equally between Oronte & Cléante: I give to Oronte all he desires from me for his sexual pleasure, even things that I do not get any benefit from in return; & from Cléante, I ask for the things that satisfy me. The one commands me, I command the other: my husband does whatever he pleases with my body; I do whatever I please with my lover's; I obey Oronte, I command Cléante. Reflect for an instant on the difference of condition between a woman who is a master, & one who is a slave; & keep in mind, my child, that to live a truly happy life, one must combine the two lives.

Octavie.

What! one cannot be happy except by abandoning herself in this way? God forfend that I should commit the least error in this manner!

Tullie.

Octavie, do you remember the dream I interpreted for you?

Octavie.

Of course; but you can also remember the protestations I made, to be always faithful to my dear Pamphile.

Tullie.

What! are you so temerarious as to run counter to your destiny; that is, to wage war on Heaven, & to imagine that you can overcome by your obstinacy what the Gods have resolved on?

Octavie.

Really, Tullie, how can you want to involve me in this kind of a life, which is so detestable? Would you have me trample on the honorable feelings that a young bride like me should have? No, you can't be serious, & what you just told me about Cléante does not seem at all like the truth: I think you are too smart for that. You must be pulling my leg.

Tullie.

And myself, I think that you are the most foolish woman in the world; & you are infatuated with certain maxims that displease me to the nth degree. Will you be content, if I made you understand how you can conceive of happiness by the enjoyment of sexual pleasure?

Octavie.

Assuredly; but I cannot imagine you will get very far: for how to reconcile in the same subject two things that are at odds & contrary to each other?

Tullie.

To instruct you in this truth, which seems like a paradox to you, know that men of today have made new laws, & they introduce into the world a cult that has no relation to antiquity. The virtues of our fathers' generation are the vices of this one; & actions not performed in the past without recompense cannot be practiced today with impunity. Among these stable engagements, & these strange revolutions, Honor has been birthed & has occupied the greater part of men's minds. Do not think, Octavie, that its existence has anything real about it. No, it has no other foundation than our imagination; & you will be taken advantage of if you think its nature should be constructed of some other matter than those objects of reason that the philosophers speak of, who owe their productions to fantasy, & which have nothing in common with reality. That beautiful, but imaginary concept was invented to hold people of our sex in a rigorous duty; it is a pure idea & a chimera, which the malice of the times obliges us to toe the line of, while wisdom dictates to us not to be attached to it. Let us feel nostalgia then, my child, along with great men, for the happiness of past centuries, when this tyrant who is in complete opposition to our pleasure was entirely unknown....

> .... *Quel Vane*
> *Nome fouza sogetto*
> *Quelli dolo d'errori, idol d'inganne*
> *Quel, che dal volgo insano*
> *HONOR poscia su detto*
> *(Che di nostra natural feo Tiranne)*
> *Non mischiavea il suo affano*
> *Fra le liete dolcesse.*

Del amaroso gregge,
Ne fu sua dura legge.
Nota a quell alme en libertate auvez ze
Ma legge aurea, è felice,
Che natura selopi, S'EIPTAGE EILIGE.

There you have it, Octavie, what honor is; that is the nature of honesty, which seduces you; judge from this if it is compatible with pleasure, & draw from this reasoning the consequences that must naturally follow from it.

Octavie.

Hmm. I see what you mean, cousin; but to satisfy me entirely, tell me why you didn't preach this honor stuff before I got married. What's the point of my abusing myself in this way, given it's nothing but a chimera?

Tullie.

The reason is this, sweetie pie. While we are girls, we are obliged to run after these visionary phantoms because we want to live happy lives. It is different once we are married: there is no more infamy for us, we have the freedom to do whatever we wish; & this fine coat that covers our amusements places us above the blackest & least sparing calumny.

Octavie.

I'm beginning to understand, Tullie; your reasons are starting to persuade me; but I still have my doubts, which you can clear up for me some other time.

Tullie.

And this is what it means to be good: to be reasonable, to let oneself be won over by reason. As for any
doubts that remain, so that they do not fatigue your
mind, I want to put you into the hands of a man who
will remove all your scruples.

Octavie.

I get it; you're talking about Cléante; but scruples
aren't put on or taken off like a nightshirt. But for
goodness' sake, my dear Tullie, tell me how you became his mistress; was he given to you, or did you acquire him by your skill; by what artifices were you
able to hide your amusements from Oronte, & finally
how did you prevent him from discovering the free-
doms you were taking to his prejudice?

Tullie.

I will satisfy you, my little love: I will tell you all
these surprising things, in which your mother played
a large part, but which you are ignorant of, obviously.
You should know then that a little while after Sempronie got married, she asked her mother to let her
keep Joconde in her service: she begged her to make
Pamphile agree, which she did; he consented without
difficulty & thought nothing more about it other than
the company they planned to keep.

Octavie.

Six months ago, Joconde got married; & in spite of
that he continues to live at the house; clearly, it's a
bias in his favor for what has been going on between
them; & when I recall what I have seen & heard,
when they were together, & that they looked down on
me because of my young age, I have to agree with

you & am of your same opinion. No, I am quite sure about it: Joconde has been sleeping with my mother all this time.

Tullie.

As far as I can tell, you know almost as much about it as I do.

Octavie.

Ah, Gods! how my mother answers poorly to the idea of honor we've had about her person! She really knew how to hide her flaws under the false appearances of virtue! I often saw them laughing & talking & carrying on together, when my father was absent; Joconde was the steward of the house then. I remember, one day among others, my mother & I we were alone in a room: she was working at some embroidery, & I was playing as children do at that age, with a female cat whose ears I was pulling & lifting into the air. I remember then that Joconde entered; & after having greeted my mother, & said something very quietly into her ear, he took her by the hand; & in spite of several efforts to resist, she disappeared with him. I thought that they had exited the room, & I was delighted they had left me free to pursue what I was doing; when all of a sudden, I heard the bed creaking, & several poorly articulated sounds that my mother made, as if she were in some sort of pain. I stood still for several moments, listening; but fear seized me, & I ran quickly to the place where I heard the noise coming from, but my mother heard me, & came out laughing & stood before me, & picked me up in her arms: "What's going on?" she said to me, "my pretty little girl?" "I was afraid," I said to her, "when I heard you cry out: what's bothering you?" "It's," she responded, "that when I was leaving the room, I hit my foot against the bed with such force, that it caused me some pain." As for Joconde, I never saw him at all; he had already disappeared.

Tullie.

But after that, you discovered nothing else of their intrigues?

Octavie.

No, they avoided my presence as much as they could; & my mother took care never to do anything in front of me that might cause me to conceive a poor opinion of her. On the contrary, she did all she could to instill in my mind the idea of a wise & honest woman, whose mores were irreproachable.

Tullie.

I know; & she asked me to speak with you about these feelings of honor that you had about her, & to make you believe her the most saintly woman in the country. I believe, Octavie, that I do not need to tell you not to divulge the secret I just related to you, it was told under the strictest of confidences.

Octavie.

I would be a parricide if I didn't protect my mother's reputation, which must be dearer than life itself to her. Have no fear on that score: only, I have to tell you how she abused my simplicity. Three days before my nuptials, she gave me this talk: "After tomorrow, daughter, you will be married &, by consequence, in

Pamphile's power: right now you are pure, you are chaste, you are a virgin, & you have only a short while to remain so, in this saintly condition; it will be followed by foulness & filth, which are inseparable from the embraces of men: all the virtues that accompany virginity will abandon you soon enough; & all their advantages will leave you, unless you make an effort, some heroic action, to hold on to them. Reflect on this, my child, & consider that as there is nothing more divine than a virgin girl, there is nothing lower, viler, & more contemptible than one who has been sullied." "But what! mother," I said to her, "what do you propose I should do? If you wanted me to keep my virginity, you could put me into a convent; I would consent to it in order to please you." "No, no, daughter," she responded, "that's not what I was thinking at all; & although you would not be the only one, the love that I have for you would never allow me to bury you alive in a convent. What I'm asking you is only," she continued, "to keep your mind intact, as I have always done, & not to be affected by the filth that your body must be subjected to. It is also necessary, my dear child, in order to make a worthy oblation of your virginity, to make a sacrifice that anticipates your loss, & another that follows it." "I consent," I told her; "but what kind of sacrifice are we talking about?" "The sacrifice," she said, "that I demand of you, Octavie, has need of both your hands & mind to be performed: you must have a great deal of courage, in order to be meritorious; & I'm concerned lest you do not have enough strength for this saintly work." "No, no," I told her, "I will be as courageous as needed, don't worry about that." "I hope so, my dear child" she said to me; "promise me then that you will put up constantly with all that I deem appropriate for you to put up with." I promised. "Eh, well, my girl," she continued, "given you desire to be as wise & as good as you are beautiful & kind, we will make this sacrifice tomorrow, after you have renewed in church the promise you just made to me.

Tullie.

Really, you are not telling me anything new. Sempronie told me this story, praising your courage a thousand times over, & laughing at the same time at your simplicity.

Octavie.

There's no need for me to continue then.

Tullie.

On the contrary, you could not make me happier than to fill me in on the particulars; because your mother only gave me an abridged version.

Octavie.

You will know then that in the morning, before I had gotten up & dressed in the richest clothes that she had prepared for me, she brought me to Father Théodore. You will easily know who I'm referring to, when you know that he is one of those fathers who affect an apparent austerity of life, & a quite particular severity of mores: one of those fathers who preach on mortification & penitence. And their beard, which they let grow, makes their face look dry & attenuated; it makes them pass for true mirrors of holiness in the minds of the people. After we had said our prayers, he came to me in a chapel where I had retired with my mother: "Eh, well, my dear girl," he said to me as he approached, "you have here a mother who will spare nothing to make you as perfect as you ought to be. You are, according to what she's told me, planning to be married in three days: you must consequently purge your soul of any defilement, to make yourself worthy of celestial grace, which cannot enter a heart soiled by the least filth. You must know," he continued, "that if you are good, the children you bring into the world will one day take the place of the fallen angels in heaven; but if contrariwise you have some bad quality in you, your children will all be infected by it & will walk down the road to perdition, to swell the ranks of miserable people. It is up to you," he said to me, "to choose." I was so ashamed that I didn't dare respond to him. "Speak," he said. "I wish," I said to him, "to be good, & that they should be good." "Come closer then. What more do you want?" I got down on my knees before him, while my mother stepped back a bit, & I confessed to him in every little detail what I thought I was guilty of. When he learnt what had happened between Pamphile & me, & that I had already enjoyed the pleasures of sex partially, he flew off into a rage. He severely reprimanded me; & after having advised me to feel a horror for my passed actions, he ordered me to obey blindly everything that my mother commanded me to do. He made a sign to her to approach; & after having drawn from his sleeve a small bundle of rope, he gave it to her without unwrapping it. "Don't spare your daughter" he told her; "be an example to her; & you, don't be so indulgent." After that, we exited the Church, & we went back to our home.

Tullie.

Do you not admire, Octavie, how these people abuse our simplicity, as they lord it over us.

Octavie.

More like how we mock them & how we hold sway. As soon as we arrived home, my mother had me enter a rather remote room of the house with her, which had no view onto the garden. She closed the door behind us & gave me, while giggling, that package of rope to unwrap; which I did, & recognized that it was a kind of whip, composed of five cords, with an infinite number of knots in it tied at various intervals. "Well! my daughter," she said, "it is with this instrument of piety that you must prepare yourself for marriage; it is supposed to serve for purgation. The good father," she continued, "ordered that we both chastise ourselves with it; I will begin, you will follow: but don't let the rigor with which I treat my body frighten you; have no fear at all & think only that, during this holy exercise of piety, my spirit will enjoy things that cannot be expressed in words."

Tullie.

You trembled with fear, no doubt, my poor child?

Octavie.

Nah, but I confess I didn't think I had it in me to endure, as I did, so rough & painful an exercise.

Tullie.

In fact, they say there is nothing so strong & constant

as a woman; when she gets it into her head to endure something, she will do it, & she will support with admirable steadfastness difficulties that would tire people with greater courage. But continue.

Octavie.

"Why waste time?" my mother said to me, giving me a peck on the cheek. "Help me get undressed," she said, "in order to uncover those vile parts of my body, which deserve all sorts of punishment." I obeyed her, & soon she was just standing in her chemise, which she lifted up over her shoulders; then, getting down on her knees, & taking the whip in hand: "Now watch, my child," she said to me, "how this instrument of penitence is employed; learn to suffer, by the example I'm about to give you." Just after she finished speaking, someone knocked at the door. I alerted her to the fact. "I know who it is," she told me, "don't be surprised; it's the good Father Théodore, who has obviously come to help us in this exercise: he told me he wouldn't miss it, if he could obtain permission to come out." He knocked a second time: "that's him," my mother said; "go open the door for him." "What?" I replied; "You want him to see you completely naked?" "Apparently you don't realize," she said to me, "that this holy man knows me inside and out, to the very bottom of my soul, & that I must not hide anything from him." She lowered her chemise nonetheless, while I opened the door. The father entered immediately, & then proceeded to praise my mother for the good example she was setting for me. He then gave a short talk on the subject, but with such force & energy, that it wasn't long before I was begging him to treat me with all the rigor he could muster.

Tullie.

Oh God! Were you out of your mind?

Octavie.

You would have had a hard time not following suit, & he would have persuaded you too without a doubt. He proved to us by polished, & apparently studied, rhetoric that virginity without mortification & penitence were not at all meritorious; that it was only a dry & sterile virtue; & that if it wasn't accompanied by some voluntary punishment, there was nothing viler & more contemptible. "Clearly, those," he continued, "who get naked before men in order to prostitute themselves to their desire ought to turn red with shame; but contrariwise, others are laudable, when they do it with a sense of piety & penitence. If you consider the actions of the former, you will find nothing but infamy; & if you direct your eyes to the latter, you will notice they embody all kinds of honesty: the first group can only satisfy mortals, but the second are capable of charming Gods. Above all," he continued, "these sorts of chastisement are widely practiced, when one knows when to use them at the right time; they are like a fountainhead, whose miraculous water possesses the virtue of cleansing women of every sort of filth they might have contracted: there is no other way to be purged, except by suffering the penitence that is imposed on them with as much steadfastness & patience as the pleasure they enjoyed sensuously that was forbidden them. Finally," he said to us, "it is in this way our souls are purged of an infinity of faults & crimes that shame & modesty often forbid us from disclosing on account of our orgasms."

Tullie.

O what a pleasant moral story! Ah! My how his precepts are engaging, no?

Octavie.

After these talks, he took the whip in hand: my mother got down on her knees; I stood back a bit, with my eyes glued on her. Having gotten into position, she begged Father Théodore to begin his "holy work" (those were her words). She had barely pronounced the last word when he unleashed a hailstorm of blows on her backside, which was uncovered: he struck it again a little more lightly; but finally he put her in such a state that her buns, which earlier were very white & polished, turned red as fire, & I was horrified to look on them.

Tullie.

Well, well, what do you know! She did not complain at all?

Octavie.

Far from it; she seemed insensitive to it; only once did she let out a sigh, saying, "Ah, my father!" But that executor of divine justice got upset. "Where is your courage?" he replied; "You're giving a fine example of weakness to your daughter!" He commanded her then to bow her head & torso down to the floor: she did it; never had she looked more beautiful. Her buttocks were so exposed, that not a single stroke missed its target. That lasted for about a quarter of an hour, after which the father said to her: "That's enough. Get up. Your spirit should be satisfied now." She got up & came over to me. "Eh, well, my daughter," she said to me, embracing me, "It's your turn now, & you must show him that you have courage." "I hope," I said to her, "he does not miss a stroke; what do I need to do?" "Prepare your daughter for this act of piety," said the father; "I hope she will be even stronger than you were." Meanwhile, I kept my eyes lowered & didn't say a word. "Will you answer to my attempt?" he asked me; "I will try," I replied. At the same time my mother was undressing me; the only thing I still had on was my chemise, which she pulled up over my shoulders. As soon as I felt myself naked, for modesty I put my face in my hands; I wanted to get down on my knees. "That won't be necessary," my mother said to me, "stand up straight." "Well, Octavie, do you want to be happy?" the father asked me, "& put yourself on the right path to Heaven?" "I do," I said. He then whipped me several times, but so gently that it tickled more than it hurt. "Do you think you could endure something stronger?" he continued. My mother answered for me: "Let her have it." Immediately, from top to bottom, I felt myself overwhelmed with blows; but they were so violent that I couldn't help crying out loud: "Ah! that's enough, that's enough, have pity on me, mother." "Show some courage," she said to me. "Do you want to do the rest on your own?" my mother asked me. "Excellent idea," said Father Théodore; "let's see how she performs. Here," he said to me, "take this holy instrument of penitence; chastise yourself, as is necessary, that part of your body that is the seat of vile pleasure." My mother showed me how to hold the whip: I gave myself two or three rather strong blows; but I couldn't continue. "I can't," I said, "do harm to myself; if you want, I am ready to take whatever you give, mother." On saying this, I handed the whip to her. She gave it to Father Théodore, because, she said, I would earn more merit at his hands, than at any other's. He started in again, murmuring between his teeth I don't know what prayer; I was crying; I was sighing; with each stroke he administered, my buttocks was twitching in a strange fashion. Finally, he wore me down, I could not stop myself: I ran from one end of the room to the other, trying to avoid the blows. "I can't take it any more," I shouted, "this work is beyond my strength." "Say rather," he said, "that you are a coward & lack heart; are you not ashamed of yourself, to be the daughter of so courageous a mother, & to act with such weakness?" "Obey him," said my mother to me: "Alright," I responded, "have it your way. Immediately she bound my hands with a silk rope, because I was using them to protect my buns from the blows; then she laid me gently down on the bed: I could no longer defend myself, & like this I was whipped properly. While Father Théodore was beating me in this way, she was kissing me: "Courage, my daughter," she said to me; "this holy work will soon be over; & the more blows you get, the more merit you will rack up." Finally, this great priest finished the ceremony. "Now, that's nice," he said; "the victim is all covered in blood, so the sacrifice might be agreeable."

Tullie.

Ah, Gods! What a sacrifice! Or rather, what cruelty! What butchery! & what an executioner!

Octavie.

When it was over, my mother unbound my hands & praised me to high heaven for what I had endured, she said; for what I had suffered so patiently, such rough treatment for a girl like me. Father Théodore also had a few kind words for me, & after having got me to commit to similar sacrifice, in the future, once I lost my virginity, he left. After he left, my mother hugged me with great feeling: "Now, you must, daughter," she said to me, "pretend to be ill with a headache, in order to get the proper rest you need. As for me," she continued, "I'm used to these sorts of exercises, & I'm no longer put out by them. She helped me to clean my buttocks with rose-scented water; then she left, telling me to get some rest, & that she'd come back in two hours to check in on me.

Tullie.

Do you know where she went, & what she did while you slept?

Octavie.

No, I don't. As for me, I couldn't be still for a single moment; because my buns were stinging me something awful, I couldn't stay in the same position for long without turning this way or that.

Tullie.

O! How happy you would have been, if fate had let you enjoy Pamphile's embraces at that moment. Sempronie knew how to take advantage of the time, &

sent for Joconde, whom she had enjoined continence on for several days. That's why he came immediately. He found your mother lying on a bed, pretending to be asleep; but he woke her up easily: he threw his arms around her neck, kissed her, touched her, fondled her everywhere; she, for her part, took him in a way that he could not resist: what more do you want me to say? They did the full monty & enjoyed themselves royally.

Octavie.

How do you know these things, which apparently must have happened in secret?

Tullie.

Your mother herself, she confided in me, & told me everything that happened down to the last detail. Joconde took three romps in the course of one hour, & Sempronie came seven times. She was afraid you might have heard something coming from her room, which was next to yours, particularly when, in an excess of pleasure, she cried out loud several times: "Courage, push, bad boy, more, ah! I'm dying, I can't take it anymore!"

Octavie.

Actually, I heard that; but I couldn't imagine what the cause of it was, or that Joconde was involved. You know he's been married for six months now, & that he married a very beautiful & very lovely young person, sixteen years old, who was the natural daughter of my grandfather.

Tullie.

Tell me again that she is the best child in the world; but for all that she is also the unhappyiest, because your mother deprives her of the pleasures owed to her by natural right.

Octavie.

I have often seen my mother blaming her & reprimanding her on account of her birth. "A girl," she said, "born like you are of an infamous love affair, will easily follow in the footsteps of her mother." She never responded, except by sobs & tears.

Tullie.

You know that Julie (that is her name) was living with the nuns, where Thérèse, her aunt, is the Mother Superior; when Joconde, who was looking to settle down, complained to Sempronie that he had not yet received any salary for all his services. "I'm entirely devoted to you," he told her; "but what have I received in return that could make me believe I have the honor of serving you? What attention have you paid to my fortune, you who know that I sacrifice myself entirely for you. If fate should take you away, what would become of me? Besides the extreme displeasure that I would have, having lost what I would rather keep, I would be plunged back into an extreme poverty." "Chill out," Sempronie said to him: "I will put everything in order; I have a plan to marry you to a girl who is rather beautiful & rather rich, – you could not wish for anyone more accomplished. I will provide her with a dowry myself, & I will do it in such a way that you will have occasion to praise me for my liberality. I have," she continued, "six thousand ecus of gold in my cabinet, which my husband has no idea about; I will put them into your hands now, if you want." "I'm infinitely obliged to you," said Joconde, "& I will never forget such considerable beneficence: I put myself," he continued, "entirely at your discretion; do with me what you will, there is nothing I would not do to please you." "You know Julie," responded Sempronie, "who I had placed at an early age with the nuns: she's the one I have destined for you; there is no one more beautiful or wiser than that child." Joconde accepted the offer with great joy, the contract was drawn up, & Julie was put into his possession.

Octavie.

Joconde has already been steward of the household for several years now, & has taken good care of all our property, both in the city & in the country. My father has always praised him for his behavior, & I am not at all surprised to learn he received Julie's hand in marriage in recompense for his services. But what were the stipulations of the contract?

Tullie.

The stipulations were that the six thousand ecus of gold would be paid in four years. That they would be waiting for him, but placed with a merchant, who would disburse them, at the expiry date, into Joconde's hands; that he would receive however the interest in the meantime, provided he kept his word as to the other articles that were agreed on for the price, & here were the conditions. First of all, that Joconde would treat Julie exactly how Sempronie judged appropriate.

That he would not consider her even as his wife, if she didn't want him to. That he would follow exactly to the letter what she commanded of him, either by word or in writing. That he would have to take care of the business of the house as before, & that he'd live in the rooms she marked out for him. Finally, that he would be entirely at her beck and call.

Octavie.

In other words, Julie was both married & widowed simultaneously.

Tullie.

You are right: because as of their first wedding night, Joconde was forbidden to ride her more than two times; Sempronie still wanted to keep the best of him for herself; & having put this new husband in the mood, he did it with her at least three times. After which she sent him back, weak & enervated, to poor Julie. The following day, she interrogated Julie, showing a great curiosity as to her health, & asked her how things had gone the night before, if she was still a virgin, or if she had lost her maidenhead. At first, Julie responded by her silence, keeping her eyes lowered & her face covered by modesty. Sempronie pressed her so much though that she confessed that her husband had enjoyed her twice. Joconde was permitted to do similarly the following night, & on the following morning, your mother had a chastity belt put on her. So that the adorable child's nether parts were placed in irons; her husband was forbidden to touch her for one full week. It was strange! From then until now, he has ridden her only fifteen times.

Octavie.

But what virtuous power can this belt have to make women chaste?

Tullie.

I will tell you. When Julie woke up at ten o'clock in the morning, Joconde entered the room with that instrument that he had received from your mother's hands: he affixed it to her; she smiled, asking him innocently what it was for. "It's something," he said, "that ought to keep you honest; it's a remedy against all the weakness of your sex, which is called the chastity belt. Sempronie, my Lady & my mistress, wore this same one for several years; & it's in this way that she acquired such a good reputation. I hope it will work out as profitably for you."

Octavie.

I've never seen one. Explain to me a bit how it's made.

Tullie.

The chastity belt that Julie wore consisted of a small gold-wire mesh, joined to four small steel chains, wrapped by thick, strong pieces of velour, two of which are placed before, & two behind. The extremities of the chains come together around the small of the back, & are attached by means of a very fine lock & key. The mesh is six inches long & three wide; so that it occupies all that space called the Perineum, that is, from the anus to the top of the opening of the vagina. It is composed of three strips that are far enough distant from each other as to allow the passage of urine, but close enough together to prevent the entrance of a small finger. Ah! Octavie, how a poor Cunt cuirassed like that is deprived of its dignity! It is really a pity!

Octavie.

Instead, you should say that it is a happy instrument, because it puts a damper on all the strange attacks that might be made against it. But what did Julie say?

Tullie.

The same thing that you will, for as I understand it, you too will be made captive soon.

Octavie.

I didn't know that. Pamphile mentioned something, a while back, about some mysterious belt. He said that there was nothing more useful for an honest woman to wear, & that my mother was advising him to have me wear one. I haven't thought about it since.

Tullie.

"What do you want me to do?" asked Julie (seeing that her husband had thrown back the covers on the bed). "Pass," he said to her, "one of your feet through these chains, & the other through those." When she had done as he asked, he lifted the belt, put the mesh in front of her vagina; & joining the ends of the small chains at the small of her back, he attached them behind her & locked them with the key. "Now," he said, "your honor is secure. You're not inconvenienced?" "No," she said, "not in the least." "Okay, then get up," said Joconde, "& walk around the room." She got up immediately & made two or three rounds about the room, not as conveniently as before, because the width of the mesh obliged her to spread her legs, to avoid harming them. "You'll get used to it as time to goes on," her husband said to her, "& it's not a surprise if that causes you a bit of discomfort in the beginning." Next he made her bend over completely; in that position of hers he looked at her attentively: he could not stop admiring the beauty of her buttocks; because it seemed to him, Octavie, that Nature had taken great pleasure in constructing her, – she was so beautiful! He attempted to slip his little finger between the mesh & her skin; but he could not, & he realized that he had nothing to fear from in front or from behind. He went promptly to go find Sempronie: "Now, Madame," he said, approaching her, "I come to bring you the two keys: but please," he continued, pulling out his hard, hot penis "enjoy this first." "I accept," said Sempronie, "& I will take it on good faith. She lifted her skirts then, & pulled up her chemise; he laid her down on a small bed, & went about his business to the satisfaction of both parties. He then had a long talk with her. "I want to tell you," she said to him, "the way in which I think you should deal with Julie; I want you to avoid all interaction with her, except as regards her having babies; as for pleasure, when you want to have some, I expect it will only be with no one else but me; that you will be both my husband, & my lover; & so that she might think that all other men act in the same way with their wives, I will give you back the key, but only every fifteen days, & you will not use it until after you have enjoyed yourself with me at least twice; for it would be dangerous if she should experience what you are capable of. As I have no doubt," she continued to say, "being as young as she is, that she has no penchant for voluptuousness; I will ask Mother Thérèse, my good friend, to reduce a little her fires by fasts & by penitences. As for you, Joconde," she continued, "if you are always constant, & if you cherish me as you have done up to now, you will see just how far it can go, the liberality of a woman who loves you; but on the contrary, if I find you to be unfaithful, & if I perceive that your love begins to cool towards me, you should consider me to be your irreconcilable enemy." "I accept these conditions," he said, "they are too advantageous for me to refuse; yes, Sempronie," he continued, "I receive them from the most lovable of all women: Julie will be your slave, I leave her in your control; & even if you want, I will not sleep with her at all." "God forbid," she said, "that I should separate in this way those whom I wanted to unite! I only ask that you alert me when you perceive that she leans to things of the flesh, so that I might set things aright by having her spend several days with the nuns where she boarded. As for the fires she stokes by her strokes, you can count on me to tamp them." There you have it, Octavie, just how far your mother's jealousy can go, she who has Joconde wrapped completely around her finger.

Octavie.

In fact, she is extreme, & I think you have lost him.

Tullie.

You are right: because Joconde loved me once, but she turned him away from me; & so that I might not have anything to complain about, she gave me Cléante instead. He is a young Gentleman, well endowed & accomplished; there is only one thing that prevents him from being esteemed equally by everyone. You should know, Octavie, that in a youthful fervor, he embraced one of the most austere obscenities being practiced at that time: he recognized some time later that his actions were a little too precipitous, & that he had fallen into a trap, while thinking he had found a treasure. He came back then to his country of origin, & quit the habit he had taken up. He then attempted to marry some woman worthy of his social standing, but that earlier change in lifestyle, which he tried to pass off as a thing of irresponsible youth, became a considerable obstacle for him; & all his great possessions & his other qualities and accomplishments, which should have made him a nice catch, were entirely useless: the truth of the matter is that the world judges things with an extreme ignorance, as if a man exiting a cloister was constructed any differently than other men. These are our minds' prejudices, that let themselves be tyrannized by usage & custom. But let us not lose sight of our subject. Cléante seeing himself thus rebuffed, stopped concerning himself with marriage; he came to this town & lodged for some time as you know with your father with whom he was allied. That was how we met, given I was coming over to your house often, hardly any days passed when we did not see each other; he pleased me at first sight, but it was his conversation that got me interested in him more than anything else. One day among others, he seemed to me more pleasant than ordinary, & his conversation charmed me: "Ah!

Madame," he said to me, "in a really engaging way, Oronte sure must be happy to have for a wife so kind a person as you! if I dared only to hope to be your friend, I would gladly prefer my condition to that of the Gods. Sempronie had not quite noticed that he loved me, & that he was not indifferent to me, when she started working to bring us together. "Ah! Tullie," she said to me; "you don't know Cléante: if you can plant your hooks into him, into his heart, just once, nothing in the world could disengage them; his constancy is as well known to me as his generosity: hating as much as he does all his relatives, his goods, which are considerable, will pass into your hands doubtless. What more could you want? a woman who finds herself desirable can feel quite sad not being loved." I gave in; & Sempronie, who took care of everything, made Cléante agree to the following conditions. That he would cede to Oronte by public instrument a portion of his possessions, & that he would declare him his sole heir in the event of dying without a beneficiary; that I, for my part, would be obliged to give him my hand, by which is meant that I would give him entire control over my body; but that it would not be put into his hands before he had first made good on his promise, by the contract just spoken of. He considered this too good to be true, – to be able to possess me at any price; that's why it did not take long before all parties involved had agreed to the conditions put forward, & that he ceded his goods according to stipulation. That same day, I found myself at Sempronie's house where he was also. As soon as he saw me, he came & threw himself down at my feet: "Ah! kind Tullie," he said to me, "allow me to take in your beauty; I kept my word, now keep yours." "That's reasonable," said Sempronie; "& if each of you recognize your respective advantages, you will live more happily than the Gods do; meanwhile, get on with your business." On saying which, she exited the room, & closed the door behind her.

Octavie.

What did Cléante do then?

Tullie.

He got up off the floor, kissed me a thousand times, fondled my tits; & defending myself like a person who really wants to be vanquished, I let him throw me on the bed: he trussed up my skirts & my chemise, & he put his right hand on my nether part. "Ah! leave me alone," I said to him; "remove your hand, you will ruin me." Meanwhile, as I was saying this, he covered my mouth with his kisses; & throwing himself on top of me, he penetrated me; he pressed me, he pushed into me, & I protested; then all of a sudden I felt the flowing of a dew with so much abundance that I can honestly say I never felt anything like it before. He did not stop there, he redoubled his jolts, & I discharged two times even during the course of his movements. Finally, he acquitted himself of his duty & made a sweet blending of his semen with my own.

Octavie.

What you have there is a veritable Hercules, as you are fond of saying.

Tullie.

You cannot tell by that alone; because after all those

major strokes, he was as vigorous as ever: I am not exaggerating, for without pulling out, he discharged for the third time. Just at this moment, I had to hold on to whatever modesty I had left, but I could not retain my grasp any longer; I forgot who I was; & as if totally transported, I lifted my buttocks & my thighs up off the bed, & got off, by a thousand movements, the man who was giving me so much pleasure. He gave me a kiss; & putting a hand on my butt, he said: "I get the impression, my dear Tullie, that you are beginning to feel something; courage, girl, give it up." "I can't," I told him, "I'm beside myself, I'm dying, help me." And on saying that, I came. Cléante could feel it; & after having redoubled his attacks, he also joined in the pleasure; & we died in each others arms, remaining motionless for a long time after that.

Octavie.

Ah! you're getting me excited by this story! It's as if I was a participant, I'm all wet.

Tullie.

Cléante, after having recovered from his ecstasy, gave me a kiss & told me that he did not give up his assault after such small attacks, & that I would have reason to complain if he did not show more vigor with so lovable a person as I was. I wanted to get up, but I found myself so feeble, that I had need of his assistance to get on my feet. "Ah! I cannot go on," I said to him, "You have worn me out so much that I cannot walk; I fear even that my strength will fail me completely, before I can get back home." "It's nothing," he said; "All you need is a little rest; as for me," he continued, "I feel fresh & strapping, & ready to do it all over again." When he had finished talking, my mother came into the room laughing, & singing a somewhat ribald song. "Well, well," she said to us, "have you come to some sort of agreement? Is your business concluded?" "Ah! I can't go on," I told her, "I wouldn't be able to keep it up..." "That's nothing," my mother said; "How did you find Tullie?" she said to Cléante, "did she please you in bed?" "Of course," he replied, "& she would be to the liking of the most delicate of men. I don't think," he continued, "that one could enjoy a more perfect pleasure than what she gave me; I discovered in her everything that sensual delight can offer, of the sweetest & most piquant sort." "And you, Tullie, what say you," she responded, approaching me. "He pleased me, to be sure," I said; "But I'm upset with him for having broken my back & exhausted me so much; I can barely take three steps." She could only laugh at my complaining, & asked Cléante to retire, so that I could get a little rest. She accompanied him to the door, after having taken leave of me & given me a kiss. "At present," she said to him in a hushed voice, "I want you to tell me your feelings for Tullie; speak freely, I won't say a thing to her." "Alas!" he responded, "I have nothing new to report on that topic; she exceeded all my expectations; she is even more lovely than I could imagine: she's got the most beautiful body imaginable; her mind is no less charming: in sum, I owe you a thousand thanks for, because of you, I now possess so accomplished a person. Try to help me," he continued, "to spend more time with her today." She told him that Oronte was supposed to dine at your house that day & that by consequence I would be resting until evening. After that, she came to me; I asked her about her conversation with Cléante: she told me everything he said; I was not upset to hear it; then she left me, to let me get some sleep.

Octavie.

Did you find it easy to fall asleep?

Tullie.

No; & as soon as I had closed my eyes, Sempronie returned with a rather ample snack. "Get up," she said, "& try to regain your strength." I got up, & drank, & ate so much, that I was completely restored. One hour later, we heard someone knocking at the door; it was Cléante who, on entering, greeted us quite seriously, because there were several domestics present: my mother found a means to make them disappear by assigning some task to them, & we remained there just the three of us. "So," said your mother, beginning the conversation, "it's important now that you think about how to take just measures in order to live happily together for the rest of your days; because if Oronte should acquire the least shadow of a suspicion about your pastimes, all will be lost." "If Tullie," responded Cléante, "wants to act in accordance with my counsels, we will have nothing to fear from her husband, even if he should be the most knowledgeable of men." "I'm all ears," I said to him, "& I will follow what you advise on this topic." "I know," he continued, "Oronte's mind perfectly; he is neither good, nor bad, but susceptible to all sorts of impressions. I want to get the upper hand on him a little in such a manner, that he will have no better friend in the world than me: I will penetrate his most hidden thoughts, & I will manage him so well that he will take me into his most secret confidences. Finally, Tullie," he continued, "leave everything to me, & have no fear; merely take care not to say or do anything that could give him the least suspicion of our pastimes." "I will play my part well," I said to him, "it is enough to tell you that I will be obedient." "Eh, well," he replied, "give me some sort of proof of that for the time being: embrace me;" "I really want to," I said to him. "I'm asking for perfect pleasure," he said. I said nothing in response. "What! Will you refuse me like this?" he said. "Exercise your right," said Sempronie; "do you want her to climb onto you herself in bed? Don't worry: I'll stand guard at the door." As soon as she had retired, he had me lie on my back on the bed; & throwing himself on me, he fucked me. "Ah! my dear Tullie," he said to me, "show me now that you love me." "Haven't I already shown you enough, by submitting to all your inordinate desires." "Play your part then," he continued. "I will, don't worry," I told him. He then pushed with such vigor, & I responded to him so well, with the movements of my buttocks, that he was brought to the moment of pleasure in no time: he gave me a sign by kissing me; I excited him once again, & he discharged; & I was so excited by the flowing semen that I followed it up shortly by my own. "Ah! I cannot take it any longer," I was saying to him, "I'm dying, ah! ah, ah..." Sempronie interrupted us: "Hurry up," she cried to us, "I hear Oronte coming up." With a thrust of my ass, I immediately threw my knight off. Alas! the poor child had not finished; some drops of that divine rain fell out onto the bedsheets when he pulled himself out of me. One moment later, your mother came back into the room & said to us: "It's nothing, don't be afraid, I was mistaken; keep at it." No sooner said than done. Cléante climbed back up on top of me; & after several jolts, he discharged as if for the first time; & I think that if it was not for Sempronie, he could have gone three rounds without dismounting. "That's enough fun," she said to us; "you'll find her even better some other time, if you leave her desiring more. She then attended to my clothes & my hair, for fear that someone might notice something amiss, that revealed our frolics. There you have it, Octavie, that is how our "nuptials" were consecrated at your mother's house; I owe to your mother all the pleasures I have enjoyed since then, with the man she gave to me. He is a Hercules in strength & an Adonis in beauty; he is a good man, civil, agreeable in everything he says; & what is more, free of all those opinions that subjugate us to so many mysteries: even though I love him a bunch, I will never be jealous of him, & I would even be okay with your spending some time with him in bed.

Octavie.

Excellent, excellent, when the holidays roll around, we'll make the best of it: but keep on with your story.

Tullie.

We dined together, Oronte, Cléante, & I; it was not at all extraordinary company. I will not tell you what we talked about; but you should know that as soon as Oronte & I were back home, he was giving a panegyric about Cléante. He told me that he found him to be a right honest man, very civil, quite spiritual even (that was his word), & that he felt a very strong inclination to become good friends with him. Meanwhile, as Venus follows closely behind Bacchus, he got excited at the sight of my breasts, which he noticed when I was getting undressed to get ready for bed. He took me into his hands, & he made me follow him into his room: "It's important," he said to me, "my dear Tullie, that this place be consecrated as well to Venus as to the Muses. After which, without any other ceremony, he hitched up my nightgown & fucked me; he pressed, he pushed, he thrust, & holding my ass in both his hands, he pulled them apart with such force, & moved them up & down with such precipitous movements, that I was the first to come. "Ah! hurry up," I said to him, "I cannot go on, you are making me die with pleasure." He obeyed me, & did his duty as well one could wish from him. When the business was over, he made me sit down beside him, & gave me this talk: "I want," he said, "my dear child, that we acknowledge something together now." "Okay," I said, "I agree in advance to whatever you want; you know me: that I'm entirely yours, to do with as you will; that's why you need only open your mouth & tell me what you desire of me, & it will be done." "I know," he said to me, "that you are very wise; & although the wisest women are not always the most chaste women, I have no doubts about your honesty: nevertheless, I fear for your virtue, unless each of us can find the means to put to the test all the weaknesses that could tarnish its shine. "Ah, what! my dear," I said to him, "why the sudden fear? What foundation do you have to be alarmed like this? That said, I do not want," I continued, "to dissuade you from your plan." "I want," he said to me, "to make you wear the chastity belt: that should not upset you. If you are wise, as I believe you are, you ought not to be against it; & if on the contrary you lacked honesty, you would see that I wanted to endow you with it." "I will suffer for you," I said to him, "whatever it is you want, & even joyfully; given I wish nothing more than to be yours only, in preference to all other men, whom I hold in aversion, or whom I despise at the very least; I promise you even," I continued, "not to speak anymore with Cléante; I don't even want to see him anymore." "Quite far from that," he replied, "I want you to be on familiar terms with him, courteously, & I ask you to act in such a way that neither he nor I should have any reason to complain about you; for him, that you should not treat him too rudely; & as for me, that you should not deal with him too freely. But the belt will take care of any fears we might have, & you will be allowed to do anything you like as long as you are wearing it: until we get it on you, I will not be upset if you avoided him altogether." After that, he measured me for the belt, with a cord of silk; & to flatter me a little, he said, "I will act, my dear, in such a way that you will have good reason to praise me, at the very moment when it would seem that I'm insulting you. The chains that will keep your honor captive will be made of gold; the mesh, which will be like a door to the palace of love, will be made of the same material, but even more, it will be decorated & enriched with a lot of precious stones, by which one can judge the worth of a slave, by the inestimable price of her shackles. I have chosen Dominico for a gold-smith; he's the best man in town & he's much obliged to me. I asked him when it would be ready; he told me that he hoped it would be ready in two weeks." After which we went to bed together, & he did me three more times that night, rather vigorously.

Octavie.

My how Venus loves you, to favor you nine times with her caresses, in so short a time span! But did you have enough energy to put up with so many assaults courageously?

Tullie.

Of course. Seeing that Oronte on the third time around could barely squirt, I pushed him & shook him so intensely, that he did his honor, not as well as ear-lier; but what do you want? From a poor payer one takes what one can get. Sempronie came to see me the following day, & I recounted to her all that had happened, but I begged her to warn Cléante.

Octavie.

He had no commerce with you then that day?

Tullie.

Not just that day, but for one entire week, we had not the least conversation, & for good reason, because Oronte was always watching us, not to mention sever-al trusted domestics of his. "Kiss me, Octavie; I can-not look at you without thinking of a certain gentle-man named François, who resembles you quite a bit in the face: there was no one so amiable, & I really got it on with him, being in Rome at the time, with such satisfaction; that same day I followed him up by three others, who also held their own & had their way with me.

Octavie.

O my God! you surprise me. What! You would have worn out, all by yourself, four men on the same day.

Tullie.

Of course, & I will tell you all about it some other time; but let us get back to Cléante. He visited us one day before, when Oronte mentioned that he was planning to spend several days in the country at a house we own in the Ancona marches. Cléante offered to accompany him; he was quite happy with that, to the effect that he would not remain in the city with me. They spent one week together; & Cléante know so well how to make himself master of Oronte's mind, that he could not spend one moment without him after that: Oronte opened his heart to him, & told him his innermost thoughts. Among other things, he told him that he believed himself to be quite fortunate to have a woman as wise, as honest, & as beautiful as I was. "Assuredly," said Cléante, "it's all the more an advantage for you, which is a very rare thing these days, & which few men possess. As for me," he continued, "I think that a husband can be sure of his wife's honesty by her good word; that he can rely on the efforts of his domestics to reveal anything to him; but I think that the surest method is this: to entrust the surveillance of her to a padlock. Women are weak; servants can be corrupted; but a padlock is proof against all deceits." "I agree," said Oronte, "& in fact I have already given the order to Dominico, the most famous goldsmith in town, to fabricate a belt for my Tullie." "That's a wise decision," responded Cléante; "& I'm all the more at ease, as wishing to establish a tight friendship with you, for there would no longer be anything that might get in the way of that: because I have to confess," he continued, "that as men are by and large a bit suspicious, & my being unable to avoid being in Tullie's company when visiting you, I would be concerned lest that made you extremely uncomfortable; which would have discomfited me in the extreme. But after you have fitted her out with a belt, there will be nothing more to fear from your side, & I also will have nothing to be apprehensive about on mine. What's more," he continued, "permit me to go into the city tomorrow, in order to be back here the day after, because I must receive some important letters; you know that tomorrow is mail day, & you realize that by attending to my affairs, I attend to yours." He came here on the tenth then. Oronte gave him two letters, one of which was for me, & the other was for the goldsmith, with the order to hurry up & complete the work underway. "Above all," he told him on leaving, "keep it a secret; for Tullie would die of displeasure if she thought I would have disclosed my suspicions to anyone else but her." As soon as he had arrived in town, he acquitted himself of his errand to the goldsmith's; & he then came to the house, where he found me alone with Sempronie. He gave me the letter from Oronte, & acquainted us with the plan that he had underway. He jested with me on the subject: I told him that he had other things to be afflicted with, if he loved me, than to be rejoicing over the slavery I was going to be put into. "Ah! my dear Tullie," he exclaimed, "totally transported with joy, I am the happiest man alive." "What good news do you have for me?" I asked him. "Listen then," he said, "for you have a part to play in all this. While," he continued, "I was at the goldsmith's, I had enough adroitness to be able to divert him from his work, & to impress into the wax the shape of the key of the lock that was to be prepared, without him noticing it." "Ah! what luck!" said Sempronie; "it's the true means by which you two are to live happily ever after together: you will have the possession of Oronte's thoughts, & you will have the enjoyment of Tullie's body." Cléante then informed us of the measures he had taken to insinuate himself so securely into the good graces of my husband. I was surprised that he had succeeded so easily, because Oronte is rather enlightened. "Enough with such discourse," interrupted Sempronie: "soup is on the table & I'm planning to sleep with you later, Tullie." "What am I going to do then?" said Cléante. "Don't worry," she said, "we'll work something out."

Octavie.

He slept, doubtless, between the two of you, & you both had a taste of him, am I right?

Tullie.

No, you are mistaken, because your mother had brought her belt along; & your father, who had exited in the morning with Joconde, in order to visit Verona, had brought the key with him. Initially, Cléante was led to a particular suite of rooms; but after everyone had gone to bed, he came to find us, according to plan. He approached the bed, on the side where I was lying, & at the same time he gave me a kiss. I will not tell you, Octavie, all the crazy, playful things he did with me while your mother was there: know only this, that he and I enjoyed ourselves as many as ten times.

Octavie.

O, for the love of Venus! You surprise me: & Pamphile, the first night of our honeymoon, had barely done it three times.

Tullie.

Oronte once did it eight times in one night. Joconde also with your mother. But that is nothing compared to Cléante, who has an inexhaustible source of semen that never dries up, & he is also as vigorous in the last cavalcade as he is in the first.

Octavie.

Was my mother sleeping during all that time Cléante was in bed with you? Or was she keeping tabs on the assault, without participating?

Tullie.

She had reason to be content from the night before, when her husband had rode her six times, & Joconde three times when his turn came, before departing with your father in the morning. So nine times the night before: that is not bad.

Octavie.

What was poor Julie doing then, all this time?

Tullie.

I will tell you, after you tell me what became of poor Octavie after she was deflowered; for I am really afraid for her; Father Théodore gives me the willies.

Octavie.

Ah, ah, ah! you're right to remind me.

Tullie.

You are laughing: which is to say that you did not keep your promise, & that the loss of your maidenhead was not followed up by any ceremony? It was not whipped into shape at all?

Octavie.

You're wrong, the sacrifice was performed: but what was amusing about it all was that the pain he inflicted on me made me enjoy my pleasure later that day with more sensibility. You should know, Tullie, that three days later, my mother reminded me of the vow I had made when I was under Father Théodore's thumb: "Have you thought," she said to me, "about performing the funeral rites for your virginity?" "Yes, my mother," I said to her, "& I will acquit myself of these last duties, as promised, whenever you wish." She took me at my word, & without putting it off any longer, we went to go find Father Théodore. He told us to come back in the evening; we did: & he had us enter a kind of out-of-the-way chapel, which had no communication whatsoever with the outside; he shut the door behind us, & told us not to be afraid, because he was master of the place. After which, he gave us a discourse on the benefits of penitence, & on the great advantages that one gained thereby; he kept his eyes lowered, his head uncovered, & spoke with such a passion, that it seemed as though he believed everything he was saying. That really moved me, & I thought that I would have willingly sacrificed my life, if he had commanded me to. As soon as he saw me thus disposed by his exhortations, to suffer all that he deemed appropriate to have me endure, he told me that my mother would serve as an example. I was so carried away that I was more afraid for her than for myself: "It is not necessary at all," I said to him, "I'm the only guilty party here, & my mother played no part whatsoever in my losing my virginity." "You will excuse me," she said, "as I have already agreed to it, aside from the fact that I won't be bothered if you received all the merit."

Tullie.

O, what a lovely conversation!

Octavie.

"That's the kind of holy emulation I like," said Father Théodore; "We will now see which of the two of you has more courage. Meanwhile, I was helping my mother get undressed; I left her wearing her chemise, which she took off; & kneeling before the Father, she begged him not to spare her, & to punish rigorously that vile part of her body which was (according to her) more guilty than the others. He asked her where the pious instrument was that ought to punish all these crimes; she said she had forgotten it in the pocket of her clothing: she bent over to get it; & as she did I considered attentively all the beauty that this posture of hers revealed to me; I admired her white, tight, & polished buttocks; there is nothing more beautiful to see.

Tullie.

You say nothing of her beautiful slit?

Octavie.

I could hardly see it; I got a glimpse of it though. Father Théodore then, after taking the whip in hand, & mumbling I don't know what prayer between his teeth, administered his blows with such violence, that it would have been able to change my resolve, if I had not remained quite constant. "Bend over," he said to her, "so that that part of your body that the law of marriage subjects to a thousand defilements receives the punishment that it deserves." She obeyed, & her body position gave me a clear view of her vagina: I looked at it with an extraordinary curiosity. It was covered with small, dark brown, curly hair; the slit in the middle was crimson; & the *Mons pubis* that surrounded it was of such an elevation that Venus herself would have desired it. That adorable part of her body was exposed to punishments as if it were a criminal, & the executioner in disguise maltreated it with such unprecedented cruelty. "Ah, ah, ah!" she shouted out as soon as it was bleeding, "ah! I cannot take any more of this; my heart fails me; a little respite; you are striking me too roughly: I cannot take it." "You're mocking me," he said, & he continued beating her with the same vigor. She didn't move, she didn't change posture; she let out only several sighs, & sobs, & shed tears. "Stand up straight now," he said to her; she got up, & I was quite surprised to see this holy man go & stand close to her, beside her; I had no idea why.

Tullie.

That holy man! you mean that executioner, because the blood, tears, sobs, & sighs of a person as lovable as Sempronie were incapable of softening him. He is a monster.

Octavie.

In fact, it seems like he wasn't affected by it in any way; because the only reason he drew near to her was to see his work close up, & to affect her more keenly. Finally, this great work was over, the had tempest subsided, & my mother after having kissed the ground, got up & got dressed. "It's your turn now, my daughter," she said to me. "I'm getting ready," I told her. She helped me get undressed, & lifted my chemise over my head: "Be brave," she continued, & remember that the more you suffer, the more pleasure you will enjoy too." "I will try," I said, "& willingly endure all the blows I receive from you." "It's not me who's going to be whipping you," she replied; "it's Father Théodore; & you will be much more worthy to receive this mortification from a holy man than from me, who am a sinner like you. Do you want me to bind your hands," she continued, "in order to prevent you from getting in the way of this holy exercise?" "Okay," I said. No sooner said than done, & I had no way to protect myself now.

Tullie.

The dirty old man must have looked you over with his eyes though, right?

Octavie.

I have no doubt about it. "I want," he said to me, "to find out now, which one of you two is the braver: I will know by your silence; & the one who can suffer without complaining about it will be the victor." After that he manhandled my buns, opening them several times & then closing them; then he pinched me in two places, with his fingertips; it was all I could do not to make a sound, which I stifled internally. That was not all: he put his hands between my legs & fondled my vagina first with one hand & then the other; I thought he would never stop: he was totally aroused by it, & finally he pulled four or five of my pubic hairs out, with a kind of violence: I stood still the whole time, not saying a word.

Tullie.

You are strong, Octavie!

Octavie.

He did the same thing to my mother: he made her lift up her skirts, she didn't mind; & after having ogled her & fondled her on every side, he pulled out several pubic hairs, as he had done to me; she trembled, & retracted her buns extremely quickly, when he buried his fingernails into them: however, she didn't say a word.

Tullie.

Get to the point.

Octavie.

What more do you want? I was whipped, he made me

bloody, & after which we returned home. As I entered the house, my mother asked me how I was holding up. "Not too well," I told her; "my ass stings in a strange way; it feels like I'm covered with ants: I'm all on fire." "That's good: so much the better," she responded; "I feel the same, & all this pain will soon turn into pleasure. When you get to your room, lie down on your bed, & pretend that you have a headache; I will send Pamphile in to visit with you in a bit; he'll heal you; but I want you to promise me that you'll tell me all about it later." I promised her, & she retired to her room. As soon as I had lain down, my husband entered the room. "So," he said to me, "my dear child; I heard you weren't feeling well?" "Obviously," I replied, "because I heard that you were upset with me." "Me, upset!?" he said: "far from it; I love you with all my heart; & to show you I'm not fibbing about it, I will prove it to you." He did what he said: he climbed onto the bed, undid his breeches, pulled out his consoling prick, & he had me hold it in my hand; I got it hard quickly, he pulled up my skirts, & then he jumped on me. Can you believe it, Tullie? As soon as he penetrated me, I was coming, but so abundantly, that I swear to you I've never felt such pleasure in my life. In a word, I discharged three times at that same moment, or rather it was one continual discharge, accompanied by so sweet a stimulation that I cannot express it. And that's not all: because when Pamphile had done his duty, don't think for a minute that my flaming desires were extinguished; no, he rekindled them; & even after he had finished & pulled his cock out of me, the mere touch of his hand on my flesh when he was drying me made me come again, & I discharged such a profusion of that divine liquor that I was ecstatic with pleasure.

Tullie.

Good to know. But there is nothing in any of this that surprises me: because the most subtle spirits of our body being attracted by the blows of the whip, together with the hottest parts of our blood, – it is only natural that they should be drawn to the places where they have more sympathy & rapport, & that they cause by their ardor an extraordinary stimulation. The Duchess Pulchérie, so commendable in both mind & beauty, owes her pregnancy to countless blows of a stick, without which she would still be sterile. The Duke Alexandre, her husband, loves her to a distraction, & he was extremely displeased that she could not have children: he tried all sorts of cures, but they were all pointless, until an Arabic doctor told him that the only way he could make his wife fecund was to whip her as hard as he could. He accepted this as oracular; the duchess consented, & the execution of it was done by her mother. Until that day, she almost never found any pleasure in her husband's most tender caresses; but right after this medicine, when the duke drew near to her, it didn't take much for her to be withering under his touch; he could breathe on her and she would come, so extreme was the stimulation she felt; she discharged copiously; & she became pregnant after the ceremony was repeated on her two days later, which brought extraordinary joy to all the family. There are also men who can never get hard except by resorting to this artifice. The Count Ardolphe, whom you know, was reduced to this extreme measure, without which all the touching & coddling & fondling by his wife, who is very pretty mind you, all the medicinal cures, & all the spices of the Levant, – could not make him rise a single inch.

Octavie.

One must be pretty cold then. But have you experimented with this at all, & have you found someone who would render you this good office?

Tullie.

No, but I am planning to try it one day, so as to experience pleasure in every sort of way. By the way, I will be leaving town tomorrow to join Oronte, who wrote to me asking me to come & spend several days with him in the country; & I will find the means to do what I wish. I will send Cléante to you: act in such a way that he will not be displeased with you.

Octavie.

I'm not getting mixed up with him, he'll need to stand pat until you return. You forgot to tell me how Julie made out on her wedding night.

Tullie.

Alas! they proceeded in the same way as with our forefathers, that is to say, without ceremony. Her father was away, & none of her relatives were informed. Sempronie made the two lovers promise to be faithful to one another, & then she immediately led them to a place where the best part of the celebrations could transpire. Before that though, she had a long talk with Julie, & maliciously gave her several pieces of advice that would have made her hateful in her husband's eyes, if he had not known her simplicity & your mother's artifices. Sempronie then having gone up to the room where the two newlyweds were, she wanted to undress Julie, who almost did not dare lift her gaze before she was standing only in her chemise: she afterwards retired to a room where one could easily see & hear what went on inside. As soon as she had exited, Julie got down on her knees before her husband: "I won't give you any trouble," she said to him; "I will obey whatever it is you order me to do. Joconde helps her up off the floor & tells her to take off her chemise, but seeing that shame prevented her, he took it off her himself: he admired her body meanwhile, so beautiful it was; & he kisses her, fondles her tits, & finally applies himself to considering the most important part of her body; he opens her lips, he closes them, he puts his fingers inside. "Eh, eh," said Julie, timorously. He has her get onto the bed, & then he lies down beside her. She, in order to follow your Mother's counsels, takes a cushion, which she puts under her buttocks, & spreads her legs as wide as she can without waiting for him to ask her. That is not all: she then takes ahold of her husband's prick, who cannot help laughing. "What does all this mean?" he says. And at the same time, he climbs on top of her, while she does not let go of his prick, & she wanted to insert it herself where he wanted it to go. As soon as she had done this, she raises her legs as high in the air as she can, above Joconde's thighs. "Remove your hand, and lower your legs a bit" he said to her, "I will take over from here;" she removed her hand, & lowered her legs, & hugged him as strongly as she could. He pushed & he pushed; & on the fourth push, he penetrated her completely.

Octavie.

Did he find her a virgin? Did he realize she still had her maidenhead?

Tullie.

He knew, as most men know; that is to say, by relying on his wife's profession.

Octavie.

I was afraid that the way Julie was acting would make him think that she was "experienced."

Tullie.

No; he could easily tell that all these manners were a result of Sempronie's jealousy, who did her best to make his wife seem detestable in his eyes from the get-go. When that first round was completed, Joconde interrogated her: "Who would have thought," he said to Julie, "that you would be so knowledgeable on your first night? & who, I wonder, instructed you to move your butt & raise your legs as you did, & to sigh at just the right moment?" She did not respond. "Don't be afraid: tell me," he continued, "& explain to me this mystery." "I wouldn't dare," she said; "but I didn't do anything that the chastest girl that I am would not do on such an occasion." "But who told you that this was the right way to behave?" asked Joconde. "Don't ask me," she said "But I want you to tell me," he replied, "or I will come away from this bed with a bad feeling in my mind about you & your honor." "It was Sempronie who gave me these lessons, & who told me that it was the duty of a young bride to do everything that I did. However, whatever you found enjoyable in it comes from Sempronie."

Octavie.

What purpose did my mother have in abusing Julie's simplicity in this way?

Tullie.

It was to make her husband suspicious: Sempronie failed; because Julie had always struck him as a very good girl & a very honest woman.

Octavie.

You haven't finished describing how they entertained themselves.

Tullie.

As soon as Joconde's prick penetrated her, Julie raised her hand & interrupted him: "Pardon me, you are hurting me, ah, ah, ah!" & he only pushed it in harder. Having animated her by more violent jolts, she said: "Oh, oh, I'm dying... of pleasure; keep going, push, push harder."

Octavie.

Ah, ah, ah!

Tullie.

Save some of that for me... Now, Sempronie told her how to act & that as soon as she felt the slightest excitement, she should let herself go with it, & let her husband know by a thousand caresses, sighs, kisses, & the most lascivious movements of her buttocks as she could imagine, – that she was enjoying it. She did not fail: for as soon as she felt the approaches of pleasure, she moved her buns, she lifted her thighs, she responded to Joconde's pushes by such brusque movements and sighs that Venus herself would have had difficulty keeping up. Such transports led her to a supreme sense of euphoria. "Ah, ah, ah," she cried, "What am I feeling? I can't take it anymore!" Her knight pressed her as much as he could, so as to feel with her that same sweet, sensual delight that she was giving testimony to; meanwhile, she kisses him, she embraces him, & she obliges him finally to do his duty. "Ah, ah, ah, ah!" he said, rubbing Julie's buns with his two hands, heating them up. "I'm dying, my dear child, you are killing me with your movements; ah, ah!" he lost all speech here. Whatever pleasure he felt, it was due to this poor innocent girl remembering everything your mother told her to do, & she took hold at the same time, in the palm of her hand, her husband's dick, & she squeezed it so tightly that it seemed as if she wanted to draw every last drop out of it.

Octavie.

As young as she is, could she endure so a long combat without any problem?

Tullie.

Alas! there was no problem of her getting overfatigued because Joconde did not fuck her anymore that night, nor the following night, after having satisfied the two requisite rounds as laid down by your mother. So, one could say that she did not really enjoy herself to the full, but only twice in one month.

Octavie.

How's that work? For a jealous woman is known to give no quarter.

Tullie.

For the rest of the month, Joconde enjoyed himself with your mother, & finding her quite disposed to do whatever he asked, he asked her a favor. "And what is that?" she said. "Will you allow me to be a father?" "I allow it," she said. "And how can I be," he continued, "if you don't allow me to have my pleasure with Julie without restrictions? The poor child has already suffered enough, & Mother Thérèse has ill-treated her sufficiently: she deserves some pleasure." "I permit it," said Sempronie, "on the condition that this will be only for the purpose of having children: & so that you don't forget it, I want to you go one week without sex; after that, you can do with her what you please." They shook hands & struck a deal, & the chastity belt was not removed from Julie until after one week. Joconde made such good use of the time that his wife became pregnant. Sempronie believes it; & it is probable, for during this time, she was quite ill-disposed & inconvenienced by headaches that she did not complain of before.

Octavie.

I hate Thérèse, ever since I learnt that she has mistreated that poor innocent girl.

Tullie.

And I dislike your mother, because she is the source

of all her troubles. She went to see Thérèse, & during her entire visit she spoke only about the fear she had that Julie was not following her duty; that she recognized she had a great proclivity towards libertinage; & that she believed it would be necessary to mortify her a bit to improve her. Thérèse, who lent credence to her sentiments, said to your mother that she had only to send her to her. Which she did, after Sempronie had removed the chastity belt she was making her wear. As soon as Julie entered the convent, Thérèse asked her if she desired to be very chaste. "Yes," she responded. "Eh well," continued Thérèse, "in order to do that you must spend three days here in mortification & penitence, & you must endure the regular discipline that I assign to you." She consented to everything, & she was whipped by Thérèse herself on three different occasions, & on the evening of the third day she was sent back to her husband. Fortunately, Sempronie was not at home: Julie recounted to Joconde all that had happened to her: he was very upset, & promised her that he would watch out for her the next time, so that such a thing could not happen again. Then, to make it up to her, so that she might forget all the pain she had gone through, he laid her down on the bed, & gave her such a good fuck, that she never remembered any of the pain she had endured.

Octavie.

And my mother never heard anything about it?

Tullie.

No: she had not the slightest suspicion, because before she returned home, Joconde had gone out; & when he returned, he found her with Julie, whom he greeted as if he had not seen her for three months.

Octavie.

Uh, what! He didn't greet my mother at all?

Tullie.

He did; & pulling Julie aside, he told her that he had something to tell her, & that she should wait for him in her room until he came to her. She exited then, & they retired, Sempronie & Joconde, to your father's room. What more do you want me to tell you? He embraced her, & then he laid her on the bed. When they had finished, they both went to find Julie, whom they found lying in bed. "I want you to show Sempronie," Joconde told her, "just how pure & chaste you are, & that you let her put the chastity belt back on you herself." Your mother praised Julie a thousand times, & the poor child was put back into her irons.

Octavie.

It covered only one part of her body.

Tullie.

Be that as it may, she was made captive; *Pars ludicra in vincula missa est*. I want to test, Octavie, if yours is as suitable for the game as it seems it should be.

Octavie.

Cléante will share with you what he finds out, after we have had the opportunity to spend more time together.

Other Books by the Publisher

Fanchette's Pretty Little Foot by Restif de La Bretonne

Je M'Accuse... by Léon Bloy

My Hospitals & My Prisons by Paul Verlaine

Salvation Through the Jews by Léon Bloy

Words of a Demolitions Contractor by Léon Bloy

Cellulely by Paul Verlaine

Ecclesiastical Laurels by Jacques Rochette de la Morlière

Flowers of Bitumen by Émile Goudeau

Songs for Her & Odes in Her Honor by Paul Verlaine

On Huysmans' Tomb by Léon Bloy

Ten Years a Bohemian by Émile Goudeau

The Soul of Napoleon by Léon Bloy

Blood of the Poor by Léon Bloy

A Platonic Love by Paul Alexis

Theresa the Philosopher & The Carmelite Extern Nun by Marquis d'Argens & Anne-Gabriel Meusnier de Querlon

Two Novellas: Francine Cloarec's Funeral and Benjamin Rozes by Léon Hennique

The Revealer of the Globe: Christopher Columbus & His Future Beatification (Part One) by Léon Bloy

Joan of Arc and Germany by Léon Bloy

Héloïse Pajadou's Calvary by Lucien Descaves

An Immodest Proposal by Dr. Helmut Schleppend

The Pornographer by Restif de La Bretonne

Style (Theory and History) by Ernest Hello

On the Threshold of the Apocalypse: 1913-1915 by Léon Bloy

She Who Weeps (Our Lady of La Salette) by Léon Bloy

The Sylph by Claude Prosper Jolyot de Crébillon (*fils*)